LITTLE BOOK OF
FairyTales

LITTLE BOOK OF
Fairy Tales

BUCKLEY & ROSE

Dancing Bear Books Ltd.

Published by DANCING BEAR BOOKS Ltd.

United Kingdom
www.dancingbearbooks.co.uk
hello@dancingbearbooks.co.uk

Twitter @DancingBearBook
Facebook @DancingBearBooks
Instagram @DancingBearBooks

Ebook ISBN 978-1-9162100-2-8
Paperback ISBN 978-1-9162100-0-4
Hardback ISBN 978-1-9162100-1-1

First Edition

Printed and bound in Great Britain by
Clays Ltd, Elcograf S.p.A.

*To every lost soul that has ever felt as though
they are the 'other'.*

*You are not lost.
You are found.*

CONTENTS

Once Upon a Time...

Foreword

LUCY ROSE & KRISTEL BUCKLEY

THIS BOOK WELCOMES creatures of all shapes and sizes. We welcome all the outcasts and underdogs. This is the first book Dancing Bear Books has published, and hopefully not the last. We've packed these pages full of the most magical fables and fairytales we could find. There is unshakeable optimism and suffocating darkness. There is wit and charm and everything in-between. We had an amazing time selecting these incredibly talented writers and their stories and we couldn't be happier with the hard work they've given us to help make this book happen.

We started this journey because of some of the gatekeeping we experienced as writers – we believe the arts should be accessible to all and this book is a tribute to that.

And thus, we began our journey.

We still have a lot to learn and are ready to slay dragons and face challenges with a brave face and gumption that can't be thwarted. We've decided that we aren't prepared to sit and wait for representation to happen, we are going to make it ourselves.

So with this in mind: to the person living with mental health issues or disability, to the working class person trying to make ends meet, to the little Ghanaian girl who wants to be Cinderella, to the person questioning their gender or sexuality, and to all of you who feel invisible:

THE MAGIC STARTS WITH YOU

"My story is inspired by the sadness I felt while researching the extinct Irish elk. I channelled that energy into a fairy tale about escapism, where our hero is a young girl and her power is her incredible imagination."

CAOIMHÍN DE PAOR
Twitter @kevinjuly

Caoimhín is an Irish ex-pat living in Edinburgh. His new year's resolution was to write more, and he is mostly succeeding (the bar was very low). His preferred mediums are poetry, flash fiction and short stories, as he is terrified of commitment.

To Disappear

IT DIDN'T HAPPEN EVERY NIGHT.

Whenever the fog appeared, it was always faint at first, and far away. Then it began creeping towards the house through the trees like a wayward cloud. The fog would transform the woods beyond the garden into something from her nightmares. The willow trees withered and became bones at its cold touch; crows worried each other with paranoid calls and took off into the open air, leaving the grey to spread in silence.

Only then, when the fog had reached its fullest, encompassing the whole yard and beyond to the faraway hills, would the giant appear. It moved slowly, just a dark shape hidden in the mist. It would stop to inspect the house for a moment and then pass on, carrying the fog away with it. But she knew it would be back again. It always returned eventually, and each time it came a little closer to her window. Tonight, she was ready for it.

The giant stepped out through the fog for the first time, and wisps of white mist stayed wrapped around its shoulders for a moment. It locked eyes with her, and she pretended to be brave. She did not flinch away. The giant took that as an invitation. It came on, right up the garden, flattening grass and scouring the soil with hoof marks. Such was its size that it closed the gap in only a few strides. In a moment, it was upon her. It stopped with its nose so close to the glass that its hot breath streaked plumes against the windowpane. Standing with its front legs on the patio and hind legs far back in the grass, it met her eye to eye. Earlier, she had piled her thickest books and climbed them like a treacherous peak to reach and undo the old window latch. Now, mustering all her strength, she grabbed the heavy frame and hauled it high above her head, like an ant carrying a great weight. Cold air poured in through the opening, spilling over her toes and billowing her nightgown.

"I read about you in one of my books. You're extinct." She said and felt her face warming with embarrassment at how silly she sounded. "Well I mean, obviously you're... not..."

The placid facial features of the creature showed no offence, nor stirred at all.

"What's your name? Are you here for me?" And with that, it bent forward delicately, lowering its nose and bringing its branching antlers within arm's reach. She looked back toward the bedroom door. Downstairs, she could still hear the arguing.

She turned, reached out into the open and touched the horns with her fingertips. Their velvet fuzz was warm and welcome, and she used them as handles to leap the gap between them, her feet landing softly on the giant's head.

"Take me anywhere," she whispered. The Elk turned and made its way back toward the forest. She wrapped her arms around its neck, pressed her cheek to the soft fur, and closed her eyes.

"Abuse is hard, but leaving it behind can be harder. I wanted to write a narrative about the aftermath and about how messy, difficult and painful the process of growth and healing can be."

MAZ HEDGEHOG
www.mazhedgehogpoet.wordpress.com

Maz is a black bi poet and performer. Her work, which has appeared in publications like Fiyah and the 3 Drops from a Cauldron, is heavily influenced by fantasy and folklore. She's performed on stages from Edinburgh to Brighton but always loves to return home to Manchester.

Mirror Mirror

'MIRROR, MIRROR ON THE WALL.'

For a moment, Ifenna considers whispering Bloody Mary instead. That slender hand could wrap itself around her throat and squeeze. She closes her eyes, imagines her breath caught in her lungs. She feels a ghost of how it would burn, how her chest would become home to a wounded animal fighting to be free. It would fight; her body is strong and, despite everything, it wanted her to live. But Mary is stronger, and those fingers would hold fast until Ifenna's body went limp and dropped to the floor.

When the priest or a parishioner or the cleaner found her, lying with terror on her face and her eyes all white, they'd say a prayer or maybe they would scream. The police would scratch their heads, turn to the paramedics, who would turn to the pathologist, who'd explain that she'd had a heart attack. Or maybe gone into anaphylactic shock. It wouldn't explain her crushed trachea or her eyes or her twisted but not broken limbs.

Maybe a biomed student would write their dissertation on her case. Maybe she'd become a ghost story, a tragic figure haunting the church toilets. Teenage girls might start to whisper her name at sleepovers, passing the legend between them and down to younger sisters. Or maybe she'd just be forgotten, an odd occurrence that makes page 5 of The Herald and a cremation that no one attends.

'Mirror, mirror on the wall.'

She sticks to asking questions, summoning things that can't kill her unless she lets them. She misses The Good Folk and hates herself for missing them. When she left, she painted her skin with keloids for remembering.

She hasn't forgotten, there is no narcotic powerful enough to wipe the knowledge of what she did, what was done to her. But out here, in this world of billions of individuals, drifting on islands not of their making, her mind is too quiet and she is so alone. She is safe, with a hundred years of belief and birth and death hiding her and a new name no one else knows. But despite the noise and office job and daily trips to her favourite coffee place, she is always alone.

Except for now, when she can speak to Them.

She breathes, gently regulates the magic's ebb and flow and waits for crystals to form under her fingernails.

'Who is the fairest of them all?'

She gasps at the stab of quartz and thorns. The ugly, raised scars ache now, as the magic tears open her cuticles. She waits for her fingertips to turn pink, then red. She waits for 10 drops to fall from each then rinses her hands clean and submerges them in cold water. Warmth makes broken skin far too inviting. She would not give them an in, not again, never again. She waits until her hands go stiff and numb, then raises the third finger of her left hand and touches her nail to the centre of the mirror. Petty, but she has never claimed maturity.

The mirror clouds, turns cool blue and slate grey and clears. The face in the glass is hers but not, a reflection with light skin and hazel eyes. The face has dimples, bright white teeth and a pin straight bob.

'A question for a query. What is your name?' The reflection can speak without stammering, always knows what to say and has a laugh like little bells.

Her fingers blossom, fresh and red and warm. The reflection watches Ifenna submerge her hands again. Her breath quickens, shallow and needy. It smiles gently and she knows it can see her pupils blown wide and sense her throat gone dry. She clears it. Swallows. Chokes. Coughs. Tries again.

'Lily.'

The reflection wraps its lips around the name, tasting its boundaries and testing its edges. It does not show its displeasure at the lie, no hint of disappointment mars the placid arch of its brows. It reaches out of the mirror and takes her hands, slips the quartz out from under her cuticles and runs its tongue over the small cracked crystals.

'You are out of practice.'

'I have asked a question.' Her voice is harsh in comparison, a guttural hiss she refuses to pack back into her chest. She knows how this works, what their glamours can do.

The reflection sighs, an elegant exhalation that unfurls from its lungs like a sunflower in bloom.

'Therese Laufmann, Stockholm. She has hair like spun wheat and skin like fresh milk. She lifts hearts with a look and mends them with a touch. Our Queen chose her at birth and she will die before age can leave its scars on her delicately narrow forehead. You are missed.'

'I am free.'

The not a mirror image changes.

A bone white, willow thin figure clutches her chin. It looks at her, capturing her gaze with its own summer blue eyes and smiles with narrow cupid bow lips.

'And yet you call on us again? You belong amongst your betters. We entertained you, just as you did us. We adore you still, come home.' It caresses her face, leaving a silver cool trail over her broad cheeks and double chin.

Ifenna spasms and her eyes roll back into her head. She breathes, licks her always too thick lips and steps out of its grasp. She pats her hair. The twists are still in place, her edges still fuzzy. Its smile falls, its eyes squeeze shut in exquisite sorrow. It pulls its hand back into the mirror.

'Our Queen misses you. She even darkened her skin for you, remember? Made herself hideous for hours at a time, year after year. She still does. She loves you so much. Come home, please.' Its final sigh leaves sand in her throat.

The mirror clears. She swallows, twists her hands in her skirt and waits for her breathing to slow. The echoes hurt, of course they do. But pain means she's alive, this pain means she is not alone.

"This story is for every scared little monster who feels like they wandered too far from home. It's not all bad, and there's always a way back if you want it. Promise."

J. DAVID REED
www.jdavidreed.tumblr.com

UK boy with a bit of Scottish, bit of English, and a lot of missed opportunities. I started my career in writing when I was published in a poetry book in Year 8, and I've never stopped. Only recently have I started writing short stories, and New Fang was a wonderful experiment for a wonderful cause.

New Fang

A SMALL SHAPE FLEW BETWEEN the trees as the orange tones of sunset fell across the canopy of tall, dark spruce.

Fang, a cub of only a few warm, well-loved years, was sniffing out a peculiar smell that he hadn't sniffed before – not in his whole life. It didn't smell good – in fact, he wasn't sure it was smelling like something he wanted to find at all. But his little curious heart was too big, and it pulled him along nonetheless.

The tall trees around him gave homes to birds and squirrels, which made a blanket of soft noise above him, as he chased his nose between trunks and under roots. Deeper and deeper he went, always careful to keep himself tuned in to his parent's smell – they were far behind him, but he knew he could find them if he had to. Or, of course, they could find him.

Eventually, he reached a bit of a clearing, where the trees seemed to die away. There was an open space, a grove of flowers and bushes that was wide and green and *beautiful*. In the centre was a pond with a frog hopping about, and on the other side, in the distance, smoke climbed into the sky from some unseen source - but that wasn't what Fang was paying attention to. No, his little nose was dragging him out into the open after that gross, enticing smell.

There was a fallen log in the grove, a bit to the left, and as Fang approached he decided that it was the log that stank. He didn't know why - maybe trees just smelled like that when they fell over? Or maybe it was the type of tree it was. Who knows - he just had to give it the best sniffing of his little life.

He couldn't see anyone else around, so he jumped up onto the log, getting a feel for it. It felt like an ordinary log. Kind of sticky from the lichen and moss growing across it, but ordinary.

As he peered down, however, Fang saw what was on the other side of the log. The more likely culprit of the smell.

A body.

He didn't know what kind it was, exactly. But it was definitely the thing that smelled. It had red on it, and looked like it was lying on its front. Fang was about to try and turn it over, when he heard something that made his little ears prick up.

Something to his left. A twig snapped, or a leaf shifted.

Could have been the wind, he told himself, but it wasn't very convincing. He sniffed the air, and smelled something off. Then he heard voices.

'Look, he's this way. I don't know-'

Fang watched as three more of the things came out from

the tree line, and looked at him. They saw him, on the log, looking down at their dead, smelly friend, and stopped. The one at the front moved slowly, reaching for something on his back, and Fang *ran*.

'Always run – if you're unsure, or scared, or something is off, you always run home,' his mother had told him. Every day before playing, or roaming, those were the words he'd been told.

Which way was home? His nose couldn't tell – he'd gotten distracted. Now all he could smell was the dead *thing* that stank over by the log. He tried to look at what direction he'd come from, but all his eyes locked onto was the three others, running at him, pointing at him with long sticks that–

BOOM!

The ground next to Fang exploded!

He yelped, scurrying back, running for his little life. Not looking where he was going, Fang slipped at the bank of the pond, falling into the dirty water. He felt his foot drag along a stone, scraping him so hard he thought he may have cut it.

He pulled his heavy, matted weight out of the water, and could hear the things shouting at him – or each other? He couldn't tell from here, and he didn't much care. He just saw the treeline, and ran.

BOOM!

The water behind him spurted open, splashing him even more with the dirty green pond water. It threw him upwards a little, and he used the speed it gave him to scurry from the bank, back up onto the grass. His fur was wet, and his back paw stung, but he ran, picking a direction and bolting down it.

Hopefully this way is home, he thought, as the sound careened around him again.

BOOM!

A tree behind him was reduced to splinters, and he could hear the shouting again now, chasing him into the woods as Fang ran and ran and ran. He ran until he couldn't hear the shouting anymore, or the booming sounds, or the smashing of trees into dust. He ran until his paws were puckered with splinters, and the dark around him was choking, and until there was nothing around him but the smell of his own blood, the dirt, and the passing blurs of logs and bark.

At some point, after running for longer than he could remember, he saw a small, yellow dot of light between the shadows. Fang adjusted his direction, moving towards the light – whatever it was, it had to be better than the cold, dark forest.

Through the brambles and dead twigs, he rushed, until he could see another light – brighter now, and kind of square?

Oh no.

The building was human, he knew that much. Most folks built their houses into the dirt, or caves. Humans made their houses out in the open, cutting down trees for walls.

Fang slowed as he approached. He could hear his panting breath, and hoped that no one else could hear him as well.

His small ears pricked up again, searching for any, *any* sounds that might alert him to the hunters that were chasing him. Or, of course, to anyone who might be in the strange building before him.

The building was built in a clearing, but because the sun had now set and the darkness was overhead, it was hard to tell exactly how large this gap in the trees was. The light that spilled from the windows lit up a small patch of grass around the wooden structure, and showed the flowerbeds that had been dug into the ground, like a perimeter. All around the building were patches of small white flowers Fang didn't know the name of, mixed with pinks and blues of larger, more bulb-like ones.

The wood was light, and looked like it would be pleasant in the sunlight – but here, in the dark, with the yellow light spilling out into the forest, it looked foreboding. Like no one would ever dare live here. In fact, Fang couldn't come up with a single reason anyone would want to.

But the lights were on.

Fang did a quick, quiet circle of the house, and saw some chairs around the back that were facing the house, along with more flower beds. A strange structure, where two tall, thin, bare trees were standing with no leaves or branches, attached at the top by a string. Fang had been told that sometimes hunters like to hang their kills from 'kill lines' like this – but there was nothing hanging from it now.

The wind blew through the trees, whistling to him as he found himself closer to the building, peering under the base of the wood. Where the building met the uneven ground, there were a few gaps – holes between the natural and the man-made, where he thought he could slip in, if he needed to.

Just then, as he weighed up his options of trying to sneak under the house and hide, he heard a creak of wood, and footsteps.

Fang froze as a cold wave of fear fell over him.

He couldn't see the stranger, only hear them. They walked out from a door he had passed, to his left.

I could run, he thought. But he remembered the weapons the hunters had, smashing trees up when they were a distance away. They didn't have to catch you, which meant it didn't matter if he was faster than them.

But, he thought, staying perfectly still and hoping the stranger didn't round the corner, *if they're outside, it means no one is inside*. And with that, his little mind was made up.

He lifted a paw, and no one came running. So, he put his paw at the opening, and no one seemed to chase him. Gathering a little confidence, Fang dug away a small section of dirt, and still no one came to try and kill him. So far, so good.

He scrambled a little more dirt away, until he was satisfied with the gap he had made. As he pushed his head in, he knew that his head was the widest part of him – anything he could get his head through, he could fit the rest of his body.

As his back legs pushed him in, he heard footsteps again – closer. Much closer.

'Hello?' said someone.

Panicking, Fang gave up on being quiet, and allowed his claws to scratch against the wood to drag him under the house. Scratch they did, and he was certain that whoever had called out had heard him.

He didn't fancy finding out, however, and simply continued to climb into this cold, dark hiding place. His head was slightly too tall for the opening, so he had to lie his head sideways to keep moving – and he *really* wanted to keep moving.

Whatever sounds his ears could pick up from outside this place were lost amongst the grunts from his small, furred chest, and the scratches of his claws against dirt and rocks. After a few minutes, his muscles started to tire, and he felt that stinging pain from his foot again. Maybe the rush of running and hiding had masked it, but now he could feel where he had cut open his paw in that pond, slicing on the wet rocks. After all of the dead leaves, dirt and woodland he had raced through, he was smart enough to know the wound wouldn't be clean.

Usually, his Mum would embarrass him by either pinning him down or lifting him up in her strong arms to lick his wounds, or clean his muddy face. She'd stand on her hind legs – something he finds difficult – so he couldn't get away, no matter how hard he scrambled and kicked and yelped. She'd clean his little cuts or scrapes, so they would get better.

Mum wasn't here.

The space was too tight to get his leg up so he could lick it himself and it was starting to itch like crazy. Fang started to dig, using his front paws to loosen up the soil under him, and make a little pit, giving him the few extra inches he needed to breath, and lick, and rest.

Under the thick, wooden slats of the house above him, with the darkness outside, and the dirt staying still and soft under him, Fang curled up into the tightest ball he could manage. From where he rested, he could just about see out through the gap he had crawled in through - out onto the grass that was softly illuminated by yellow light.

And he saw the shadow that blocked the light for a moment. Passing, unassuming, not having seen his entrance, thankfully.

But there was definitely something out there, and it was looking for him.

Fang closed his eyes, and tried to ignore the cold and the fear and the itch on his paw. He tried to sleep.

* * *

The rumble of his own stomach made Fang stir, and the light that breached the tunnel to glare in his eyes made him greet the morning.

He'd slept, but he hadn't eaten his usual breakfast of berries and rabbit, and he felt weak for it. Dad would often hunt overnight, then sleep in on the morning, while him and Mum got to eat the spoils. His sluggish body warm and cosy, wrapping around him and Mum, like a blanket that hugged back.

His nose, like his face, was maybe the most 'human' part of him. Soft and pink skin, with only hints of fur until his hairline, that felt warm no matter the weather. This morning, his fur was all he had on his back – clothing was a treat for sleeping, to avoid getting the shivers during the night. A smell met his human nose, and his wolfish senses knew exactly what it was smelling.

'Bacon,' he said out loud, before he had a chance to stop himself.

His eyes wide, he cowered for a moment in the dirt, convinced someone would have heard him, and would come down here and do the same thing to him as had been done to the trees last night.

No one came, though. No one had heard him. No one chased him.

Allowing the thought of the hunters to fall to the back of his mind, Fang got lost in the mouth-watering stench of fat and meat that floated down from above. The smell of a delicious breakfast that would soothe the rumble in his stomach, and fill his mouth with juicy meat and maybe some juice, or something baked – like fresh bread. Oh, fresh bread would be amazing.

Knowing the risk was immense, but unable to deny himself, Fang gave in. He started to crawl back through the tunnel he had scrambled down last night. As he approached the opening, where his scratch marks had etched into the wood of the house above, he could almost taste the food he was desperate for.

But he could hear something as well. Singing... no. Not singing. Humming.

And it wasn't close. In fact, it sounded like it was really high up – if the house had two levels, the person humming must be all the way at the top. He could risk that. Get in, maybe through a window, while the person was humming. As long as he could hear them, he would know where they were – he was safe.

Fang took a deep breath, and pushed his sideways head out through the opening.

No one's here.

He kept going.

In the sunlight, the house *was* lovely. The wood was clean and light, not like the trees he was used to, which were so rough and dirty. The flowers smelled like pollen and sugar, but they didn't compare to his target.

The sky was clear blue, but for a few fluffy white clouds

that drifted over the trees. He could see now how far the treeline was – they were quite close. Maybe less than a minute's walk, less than ten seconds running. That would be fine.

Keeping his ears up, and his body low to the grass, he crawled right, the place the stranger came from. The shadow that had passed his hiding place, no doubt. *Didn't even see me, stupid*, Fang thought to himself, but he didn't risk laughing out loud. No, he had a mission that required stealth.

The door was open, and swung lightly in the breeze of the morning, letting the smell from within waft out. Fang heard his stomach make a noise, and his mouth started to water, he knew he was going to risk it.

He came up to the doorway, and risked a look inside.

The room was homely. Small, with long wooden table tops and pots and pans all over. Whoever lived here liked to cook. There was food sizzling in a pan over a stove, and Fang could hear the popping of fat in oil and *ugh* it smelled so good. A few homemade craft pieces dotted the walls, and from where he was, Fang could see an open archway that led into another room, and the bottom of a staircase.

The stranger must be up those stairs.

Fang stepped in. His front-right paw stretched into fingers, and lightly set down on the wood of the floor. It didn't creak under him as he shifted his weight, thankfully, and he relaxed a little. All he had to do was steal a bit of food, and he could eat enough to be big and strong so he could head back into the woods. Thinking of it, he wasn't *completely* sure which way home was – and he'd lost his parent's smell a long time ago – but he was confident he could try. He had to try, right?

Either way, his prey was dead ahead, frying away softly in a pan on the other side of the kitchen, over there. He snuck in, keeping low to the ground so he could hide behind a cabinet or something if the stranger came back.

As he got closer, the smell of bacon filled his nose. He almost let out a groan as he imagined taking a bite into the meat, filling his belly. Distracted, he took a slightly too-heavy step and the wood under him let out a small whine, creaking under his tiny weight.

He froze, keeping his ears tuned to the humming – it was still upstairs, and hadn't seemed to have stopped or come any closer. Continuing on, Fang soon found himself at the base of the oven, where the stove sat on top. Up there, he'd be able to steal some delicious meat, and then disappear into the treeline. Perfect.

The handles for the drawers and cupboards gave him an easy ascent up onto the cluttered table top, where sliced vegetables and cutlery were left lying about, seemingly to be organised later. The bacon was starting to burn a little, browning at the edges, giving it that slight *crisp*. Fang felt his stomach rumble as he approached, and lifted his paw to try and swipe the meat out of the pan.

Creak.

Fang froze, his ears twitching around – he'd been focused on the food. It wasn't his weight that had caused that noise, had it? Hopefully it was, and it'd go unnoticed by the humming stranger. Only... the humming had stopped. He couldn't hear the stranger any more.

Another creak of wood, and Fang looked up to the staircase, of which he could only see the bottom three steps. A foot appeared, and Fang panicked.

He smacked the handle of the pan – mostly intentionally – and watched as the meat scattered across the floor. The stranger yelped, and hurried down, but Fang wasn't paying attention now. He grabbed the bacon in his mouth, and another in his paw's fingers, then sprinted to the doorway.

'What the...' he heard from behind him, before he managed to scurry round and out of sight – he hoped. He bit down on the hot meat as he followed the side of the house until he spotted his little scratch marks, and jumped face-first into the gap between soil and wood.

Safety.

Fang pulled himself deeper into the dark, lit only by the stray rays of sunlight that managed to follow him to the small pit he had dug out for himself. He curled up, and ate the delicious meat in small bites, trying to make it last. He didn't know if he'd be able to do that again – and he was too scared to make the run across the open space between the house and the trees now that the stranger had seen him. Nightfall. He'd wait until night, and make a run for it then, once the sun had set. His mum and dad were probably looking for him by now, so they might pick up his scent and come get him before that anyway. No need to worry.

He finished the bacon, and was thinking about digging his pit a little deeper when a shadow passed over the front again – just for a second. A flash of dark, blocking the sunlight. The stranger was outside, and walking around – maybe looking for him?

He stayed still, keeping his shoulders up and his eyes wide, so he could look out into the sunlight without the stranger being able to see him back.

The shadow came back, and it stayed. Fang could see two legs, silhouetted against the bright outdoors, standing over the gap to his tunnel.

The stranger crouched, and looked in, and Fang saw the glint of their eyes in the sunlight. He yelped unintentionally, and hid below the lip of his pit to try and keep the stranger away. If he couldn't see them, maybe they couldn't see him.

A few moments passed of heavy breathing and quiet, and then the light returned. Fang risked a peek over the lip of the pit, out into the tiny tunnel, and there was no one blocking the exit. No stranger. Maybe they hadn't seen him? Or they saw the hole, but didn't realise he was still in there?

Either way, he was safe for now. Only a few hours until sunset – he could wait that out. Hopefully the bacon would be enough to keep him going.

At some point, Fang must have fallen asleep. When he awoke, it was still daytime, and he didn't know how long he'd been out, but his leg was aching and it was starting to feel really cramped under here.

He knew he couldn't risk going outside, but from his little vantage point he could see the blue flowers in the clearing, the grass, and the trees of the forest, all waiting for him to run amongst them. Running at all would be a gift – his paw still hurt if he put too much weight on the middle of it (best to run on his toes for now).

A strange, intoxicating smell weaved its way down the tunnel, however, and gave little Fang a renewed temptation to go and investigate. It was a stupid, dumb idea, based on nothing except his again-empty stomach, and cramping legs wanting to stretch, but he made it anyway. He wanted to go outside.

Fang crawled his way up to the entrance of the tunnel, and found a little surprise. There, at the mouth of his hide-away, was a plate of food.

He sniffed it.

Oh, wow, steak.

Fang licked his lips, and stuck his head just an inch or two out into the open air to take a closer look, and lo and behold – two steaks sat on a plate at the entrance to his tunnel. While obviously a trap, Fang was in no position to be turning down free food – so he darted out and grabbed the steaks in his paws, stuffed them between his teeth and, with a wide, full mouth, threw himself back under the scratched wood and into the warm dark.

He didn't see the person watching him.

Hours passed, and even though Fang made a point to make the steaks last as long as he could, he knew the meat would only last him till morning before he started to get hungry again – never mind the cold. It had been okay last night, but there were dark clouds overhead. If it started to rain, he'd never make it back to his parents. It could take all night just to sniff them out – the rain would make finding their scent almost impossible.

Usually he loved the smell of the forest during a rainstorm. He and his dad would sit under a log or in an abandoned shed somewhere, or even in their cave if the storm was bad enough, and just smell the air. The flowers and the grass would stink of pollen and spring, and the rocks would give off a timeless odour... something Fang knew how to recognise, but would never be able to describe.

For the first time, Fang let the situation shake him. He hadn't really allowed himself time to think – either he was running, or hunting, or sneaking. But now, he was just... waiting. Waiting for the dark to hide him. Waiting for the rain to come and go. Waiting for his mum to come save him.

The pup cried to himself for the first time since he had fallen from a tree, maybe a season ago. He had landed on his side, and cut his arm on a sharp branch hidden by a layer of undergrowth. He'd sat and wailed in the forest for a minute before his mum came to him and took him in her arms, back to their cave.

He didn't think that would happen this time.

In his sadness, and hoping the stranger wouldn't be able to hear him, Fang let out a small howl. Too small. His throat couldn't do it. He'd always had trouble, but now he needed it to work. He needed to call.

He let out a howl that would have made his father embarrassed for him. It was barely a call – too light, too soft, too sad. He didn't have it in him.

The yellow glow of light that was always spilling down into his tunnel faded for a moment, and Fang tried to mask his crying, but it turned into a whimper – not nearly silent enough. Fear froze him as a dark shape covered the light.

Again, the familiar smell of cooked meat filled Fang's little nose. This time, he didn't know if it was a trap or not. There was no trap last time... but maybe it was just so he'd trust the stranger.

Maybe they had one of those weapons, and they were going to turn him into splinters.

Maybe the food was poisoned, and they were going to kill him and hang him from that line.

Maybe... maybe it was just food.

He wasn't hungry right now though – those two steaks had been more than enough. But he'd be hungry by the morning, and the dark was setting in. And the rain would be harsh, he thought.

No. He didn't need the food. And he didn't trust going to get it while the stranger stood right there. If they left the food, he'd maybe go out and get it. But only then.

The shadow stayed for a few minutes, sometimes shifting or moving, but when the rain started they left. They left the food behind, though. Just there. For him.

Why?

Fang waited another few minutes – long enough to let the stranger go back inside – before even approaching the edge of the tunnel. True enough, the plate of food was still there, same as last time.

It wasn't steak this time – it looked more like bacon, but thicker. Whatever it was, Fang nabbed it with full intention to keep it with him until he got hungry again. No use leaving it out in the rain, after all.

'There!' came a yell. Fang's yellow eyes flicked up to the treeline, where he saw two emerging figures. Holding those weapons. 'Under the house!' The hunter pulled up the weapon, and pointed it at Fang, and he knew what happened next.

He gets turned to splinters.

Unless I move. Move, Fang. MOVE.

He darted off, just as the scratched wood at the mouth of his tunnel was reduced to mulch. The thick, loud *BOOM* that coursed through the air seemed to propel Fang as he made his way around the house. Past the hanging line, past the blue flowers – where the stranger was.

44

Fang saw her properly for the first time, now. In a small red dress, with white hair and a blue flower behind her ear. Her lined face was slack with shock, and the small metal thing she held in one hand slipped from her fingers as she looked at Fang.

Next to her, there was an open doorway – Fang ran to it.

The stranger started shouting now too. He heard her and the hunters yelling at each other;

'You'll do well to get off my property!'

'He's ours – where's the little half-breed?'

'I don't give a damn – you get that gun out of my face and take yourself back into the woods.'

Fang hid behind the door, on the other side of the house to where he had been last time. From where he was, all he could see was the steps going upstairs, and a corridor he knew went to the kitchen. It looked too warm, even though the rain lashed down and the hunters were still yelling.

'He's worth more than you are,' one of the hunters said, and Fang heard a *crunch*-ing sound.

Not waiting to find out what had happened, Fang ran for the stairs, going upwards. The soft, red rug was catching on his little claws, making it hard to run, but he did anyway – he had to get away. At the top of the stairs was a hallway, with some of the doors open. There was a ladder as well, going up into the ceiling, which looked like a pitch-black hole.

Fang knew how to hide in a hole.

He scurried up, hoping his claws weren't going to scratch the ladder and show where he was going, but he didn't slow either way. Up the ladder, the room opened up into a slanted-roof space filled with boxes and bags. The floor was cheap wood that bent under him, barely able to take his weight, but at least it didn't creak loud enough to be heard over the rain.

There was a window at the end that let him see out, above the yellow light that spilled from the kitchen.

He heard movement from within the house – under him, shifting and moving. The footsteps were wet-sounding, and the sound of stomping, squelching footfalls put a shiver through young Fang's body.

A hand appeared over the square hole of his hiding place, and Fang watched from the gap between two boxes as someone – it was hard to tell from this angle – emerged from the corridor beneath.

'Up there!' came a voice, bellowing, but still quite far away, and Fang realised the person who had climbed the ladder wasn't one of the hunters – it was the stranger. She was here. Why? Was she trying to find him too?

She looked around, until a flash of light from outside lit up the room. She was wearing a jacket now, spattered by the rain. Fang's eyes reflected the flash, and gave him away. The stranger came round, behind the boxes and across the thin floor, and crouched next to him.

'Can you understand me?' she asked, her voice low.

Maybe she didn't want to be found either.

Fang nodded in response.

'Okay. Those men, they're looking for you. They know you're up here – they're coming. If you hide with me, I can maybe sneak you past, understand?'

Fang nodded again. *She's going to help me.*

The stranger nodded, then turned around. She lifted the jacket she was wearing, and Fang climbed underneath, using his claws to climb up the fabric of her dress and cling on for dear life. He dug his claws in to take his weight, his back paws finding purchase on some piece of fabric with more tension, letting him hold himself flat against her back. She stood, and gasped a little as his claws scratched through her dress somewhat.

She went back to the ladder, and started to climb down, when Fang heard the hunters again.

'Where is he?' demanded the hunter. Fang couldn't see him from here, but he could hear the anger in his voice, and the soft drips of water from the rain running off him.

'I didn't see him up there. I don't know. I swear, he's just been hiding under my house for a day or two – he's good at hiding. He could be anywhere.'

The human was lying for him.

'Check up the ladder,' one of the hunters said. 'I'm going back outside.'

'I'll come,' the stranger said, as Fang clung to her back. He heard the creaking of heaving boots on the ladder, heading upwards, and away.

Fang and the stranger followed the other hunter back outside, but he was starting to slip. His claws had ripped small holes in the back of her dress, and he was starting to lose his grip. He dug into her, knowing that he was clawing flesh when he smelled the iron-tinged scent of blood as it mixed with the smell of rain and damp fur.

Fang didn't relax until he heard the rain hitting the jacket he hid under. Once he knew they were outside, he allowed himself to slip a little. The stranger came to halt somewhere, and Fang dropped from her back and to the wet grass, slicing down her back as he did so.

She couldn't help but cry out in pain, and Fang watched from behind her feet as the hunter turned. He was about to ask what was wrong before he saw Fang, and put two and two together.

He raised his weapon, but the stranger charged at him.

BOOM.

Fang watched as the stranger stumbled back, the force of the weapon sending her onto her back. The hunter, for a second, was frozen, just looking at the woman on the floor.

He felt the sadness in him, for this strange woman who had fed him, helped him, hidden him. Died for him. The emotion bubbled up, and he allowed it to release in one long, loud *howl*.

The sound erupted from his small frame, forcing its way above the sound of rain, and shouting, and the wind rushing through trees. Wailing and sad, he let it out. His first howl, for his protector.

Then it was over, and he started to run.

He had done this before, and he knew what would happen next. He would run from the hunters, and they would chase him. Or they would, usually. But, as Fang ran, he did not hear the sound of shouting, or running behind him, nor the sound of *booms* cascading across the trees.

What he did hear, from his left, was the sound of footfalls. Lots of them. Running towards the house.

Confusion clouding his little head for a second, before the scent caught his nose.

He turned, heading towards the house again, running towards the hunters and towards the onslaught of sound and smell.

He watched the yellow light, as it illuminated the shapes that erupted from the treeline. Huge, beast-like shapes that looked like wolves but stood like men, hair and skin shredded with scars and eyes full of fear and anger.

Mum and Dad.

The following events were short. The pack took care of the hunters that had chased their young so far from home. The food was good that night, under shelter from the rain and wind.

But Fang demanded they go back to the house. He wanted to give the stranger a proper burial, under the earth, in her garden of blue flowers. His protector in red.

"I wanted to write a fairytale about a girl who is happy not conforming to society's expectations, but instead embraces her differences and turns them into strengths."

ANNMARIE MCQUEEN

www.annmariemcqueen.com

Annmarie is a 25 year old creative writing graduate based in London. She works as a freelance marketer and videographer while trying to find the time to finish her novel and start an etsy shop selling soy candles. You can find her poetry account on instagram @chai_lights.

The Tigress

LAVALI WAS PRETTY SURE THAT something about her was changing. She couldn't identify what the change was, or why it was occurring, but she knew it was there. She'd always been told that she had tiger senses, the uncanny intuition of those majestic predators that ruled the Western Ghats.

As a child she'd indulged herself, tried to see the world through feline amber eyes instead of her own and prowled about the house on all fours, pouncing on her mother's carefully arranged flowers, the imported furniture, antagonising her parents to the point where they would beat her for playing such childish games.

Afterwards Arjun, forever sheltered in his position as beloved only son, would come to her room and examine the red marks that snaked up her calves. She wondered if he felt a smug sense of satisfaction, seeing this physical proof of their parents biased love. She never asked because Arjun was a good brother and she didn't want to taint that image.

He brought ointments that soothed the stinging pain, and he would hold her as the tears welled up and whisper his favourite verse into her ear:

Tiger tiger burning bright
In the forests of the night
What immortal hand or eye
Could frame thy fearful symmetry?

It was written by a brilliant Englishman named William Blake, Arjun had told her. It was far more advanced than anything he'd studied so far at school, but Arjun had always excelled at English; one night he had snuck into their father's study and stolen the verse off the top shelf.

It was found in a big, old tome; drowning in a layer of dust, abandoned and neglected for years before Arjun bestowed his love upon it. He read the book religiously, hid it under his bed and committed whole passages of it to memory, though he said he only understood parts.

Lavali didn't mind that it made no sense. She loved listening to Arjun recite, following the gentle pushes and pulls of his lilting accent and the rich, proper vowel sounds that their parents insisted upon. Enunciate. E-nun-see-ate. English sounded beautiful falling from his young boyish lips, coalescing in the air and fermenting the way Marathi never did.

When she spoke English it was clipped and harsh, brittle on her tongue, as if it had been ejected premature from her fumbling mouth.

But recently Arjun spoke less, retreated to his room after dinner and refused to answer when she knocked on his door. She would press her ear up against the hard oak and listen for signs; a breathy sigh, a frustrated thump, a slip of those unattainable English words that existed in her brother's world.

She never heard anything. Not once. Not even a hint of Blake.

Around the same time, other strange things began happening. One day, she looked up and the sky began to quiver, puffy clouds swirling into a vortex of blue, trembling as if from the force of holding itself up.

When she blinked, the trembling had stopped and nothing had changed: the streets of Mumbai thronged as usual in the midmorning heat and cows paused, placid-eyed, in the middle of roads, tail-swishing islands in a sea of frustrated traffic.

The day after, her first period came. She knew about these things from the girls at school, so she was prepared. She stayed calm. She decided not to tell her mother, and instead sourced sanitary pads herself, disguising them in the rubbish bins. She could handle three days of this.

But the blood didn't stop, and after a full week she began to grow frantic and wondered if she would die this way, bleeding from the inside out, drained of liquid until all that remained was a dry, hollow casing like the shells the cicadas left behind.

One night she dreamt of the tigress. For the first time, she was truly seeing through those feral eyes and it was vivid and real – nothing like the pretend games she'd played. Things moved in slow motion. A white-speckled doe, ears alert and pricked up, leapt through the trees with a soft rustle.

She began to follow, revelling in the rhythm of her padding footfalls, picking up speed and darting through a labyrinth of vegetation. She was hyper-aware of the forest swelling around her, alive, with its symphony of bird calls and delicate perfumes, the taste of heady, damp air, ancient tree-gurus watching silently from above.

She woke in a sweat, the taste of dewy bark still on her lips, the smell of the doe's fear kick-starting her usually dormant appetite. Somehow, without having to check, she knew that her period had finally stopped.

The dreams began to come more often after that. By day she would navigate the streets of Mumbai and masquerade as a normal school girl, but by night she would stalk the depths of the Indian jungles with her tiger eyes: hunting, exploring, ruling.

She considered telling Arjun about these wonderful dreams, but he had seemingly lost interest in her. As the years went, the distance between them grew. Now he spent his time in art-house cinemas, or discussing Victorian poetry with his 'tutors'. They loved him; they thought him a young prodigy and talked constantly about how he would go on to study at Oxford and write scholarly essays about dead poets. And though Lavali still idolised her genius brother, just as she had always done, the seeds of jealously sprouted into bitterness.

Sometimes, dreams and reality blurred into one. Flashes of the forest, the scent of blood or the sound of a running stream, would come back to her during the day and take her mind hostage. She began to notice other changes in her body; her senses were sharper than they'd ever been, she could pick up the smallest of sounds, overhear every word of her parents' arguments even from the garden.

Her vision, too, had improved. She'd always been short-sighted, but now she could see every minute detail of the world around her; the dizzying beat of a fly's wings, the colours reflected in the shiny surface of a lotus flower, the weaved strands of fabric in a woman's sari.

She began to crave meat, though she'd been a vegetarian since birth. The smell of the barbecued chilli sausage the men on the beach sold made her salivate. She skived off school to fulfil her cravings, then, full and heavy, she would explore the hidden crannies of the city, the abandoned places that belonged to no one.

Her parents were furious about her slipping grades, her unexplainable absence, her habit of daydreaming. They didn't understand that she knew already, could smell their anger, just as she could smell their fear too when, instead of submitting, she would return their screams with just as much rage.

The city felt too small to contain her. The stifling classrooms, the same monstrous roar of traffic every day that hurt her ears, the same pedlars on the street and the same women buying yams at the market.

She could see her life stretching out before her, up and out like the skyscrapers that towered over the city. A college education, perhaps a mindless job suitable for a woman of her class, an arranged marriage and children of her own.

She had to leave. She had to escape that pre-ordained future and all the obligations that came with it. Though it swarmed during the day and throughout the night, city life felt unbearably slow, trudging from past to present to future at a mechanical pace. She wanted to run. She wanted open spaces, new air and uncharted territory. She wanted trees rather than skyscrapers, a floor of crushed leaves rather than concrete. Maybe then, in the stillness of the forest, she would be able to move.

She decided to leave at night, to avoid a final bloody confrontation with her parents. She couldn't help but think that they would be glad when they woke in the morning to find her letter, that a secret part of them would be relieved to finally be rid of the daughter they'd never really wanted. The accidental daughter. The mistake daughter. The daughter with the tiger eyes, who turned out to be more tiger than girl.

It was a warm night. From the driveway she could see city lights blinking and pulsing in the distance, as if communicating with each other.

She ran her hands over the prickly spines of the roses that grew in the front garden her mother had so lovingly cultivated, caressed their dried petals and gave them a silent prayer for rain.

The front door opened with a creak.

It was Arjun, dressed in loose pants and an old shirt, reading glasses perched precociously on his nose, dark hair wild and unruly.

"Where are you going?" he asked in Marathi, their mother tongue.

"I am leaving," she replied in English. Now she could speak it too, just as well as him.

"You can't," he whispered. "Where will you go? How will you survive?"

"I will find a way. I'm more capable than you think."

"Mami and Papi will-"

"They will be glad I am gone."

"How can you say that?"

"Because it's true. You are the one they always wanted. I am a failure in their eyes, more trouble than I am worth."

He didn't try to deny it. The truth was too palpable, sitting there between them like a crouching cat. "You can't leave," he said again, and this time there was a break in his voice. "I will worry. We will all worry. I don't want you to go."

"But you will be gone too. To England, to study poets at Oxford. You won't need me here."

She could hear his heartbeat from across the gravel driveway hammering hard against his ribs, could smell his desperation.

"Where will you go?" he asked again.

"I don't know yet. I will travel around, I suppose. Go somewhere quiet and peaceful, with space to run. Somewhere with a waterfall and a good view."

"If it's about the marriage, I could talk to-"

"You can't change hundreds of years of tradition, Arjun. Just like you can't change any of those verses you love so much. It doesn't work that way."

"I would try, if it would make you stay."

She was surprised and touched by the gesture; it stirred a deep yearning in her that had lain dormant for years, a wishful nostalgia for the kind of relationship they could've had. It made her heart ache with the heaviness of it, wondering if they would still be in this position now had he said these things years ago.

"Thank you. But it's not only about that. I need to be away from the city for a while."

In the silvery light, she thought she saw a bright sheen to his eyes. "Will you come back one day?" he asked eventually.

"I think so. Perhaps by then you will be a poet yourself."

He chuckled, but it was a grating, painful sound that made her own eyes water. She didn't want to leave him, but they had become very different people.

"There's nothing I can do to change your mind, is there?"

"No. I'm sorry, Arjun."

"I should be the one apologising. I should have been

better." *A better brother to you*, was left unsaid.

He came to her then, walking across the gravel with his bare feet, and wrapped his arms around her as a crisp wind swirled around them. His tall, angular frame enveloped her slight one and she breathed in the familiar scent of him: musky, expensive cologne mixed with the smell of chapatis and ink.

Somewhere under that there was the smell of the boy he had once been, the one who healed her bruises and repeated a dead man's words to her of tigers in the night.

'*Now I am the one burning,*' she wanted to say, 'burning bright in these hidden forests.'

But maybe he knew that already, maybe she didn't have to say it.

"As a mixed race third culture kid one thing I was never raised to do is conform to society's expectations of me. I wanted to write about someone who felt the same way."

JOMA WEST

Twitter @jomawest

Joma West is a third culture writer whose work straddles both fantasy and science fiction. Joma's novella, Wild, won the 2016 MMU novella award, and was published by Sandstone Press. She has had short stories published in various anthologies.

Tin Girl

AS PER THE TRADITIONS OF MY PEOPLE, on my twelfth birthday I was placed in a tower and guarded by a dragon.

This made life smaller for me. I existed within a few rooms. I lived through books. It could have been worse, but on the other hand, it could have been better. I missed being outside, I missed people.

I wasn't always alone. I was permitted visitors, but only those approved by the state. That limited guests to blood relations. During the first year of my cloistering, visitors were frequent. Then the flow stemmed. Then it almost stopped altogether. Life moved faster beyond my walls.

The dragon, Pacu, often tried to reassure me:

'The less people see of you, the more mysterious you are. Men love mystery.'

And this was the reason I was here: to secure a noble husband — one that could get past Pacu, scale the walls of my tower and rescue me from solitude.

I always countered this statement with:

'What do dragons know of men?'

Pacu would laugh— a sound that made me think of

blades clattering and scraping against each other, a sound that reminded me of being a small child in a castle full of people.

I was terrified of the tower when I was that child. I had nightmares of it. The tower I dreamt of stretched up into the stars, an impenetrable rock so unfathomably tall. There was no way in, and yet I was in it. There was only one room and I shared it with a dragon, a snake like thing, whose face I could never see. The dragon I dreamt of would always wrap itself around me and whisper in a deep voice: 'Go to sleep'. Then it would squeeze and I was helpless in its coiling embrace.

The last time I had this nightmare was just before my twelfth birthday. When I woke up, I was wrapped in bed sheets and gasping for air. I was also bleeding.

When the day came, I was dressed and made up and brought down for the birthday breakfast. One feast was followed by another and the whole kingdom seemed to be celebrating. I was led through the meals and the ceremonies. I was manoeuvred through the dances. I was overwhelmed by the sounds and the joy that surrounded me. And then at sunset the whole world seemed to go quiet and I was overwhelmed by the silence. I tried to focus on everything I could see. I tried to learn the shades of that sunset. I tried to look into the faces of the people around me, the people celebrating me and what I thought of as my end, but no one would meet my eyes. I wondered what they knew that

I didn't.

I was put in a carriage. It was me, my father the king, and my lady mother. We said nothing as we were driven away. We said nothing for the whole journey. I remember how hard my heart beat. My palms were sweaty and I kept rubbing my hands on the skirt of my dress. Visions of that nightmare tower and that nightmare dragon blossomed in my head with the question: Why did I have to go and live in a tower? Why did I have to be taken from the world before I had had a chance to learn anything about it?

I saw the building first. That was a strange relief. It wasn't so tall. No higher than the turrets of our castle, and it was fairly squat, with space for several rooms. I saw the dragon next. That was not so much of a relief. She was different from the one I had dreamed, but she was cut from the same pattern. She was long and sinuous, longer and larger than I could have imagined, and when I took in her proportions I was sure she could wrap about the tower itself, many times over and still rear up above it. She was scaled in a multitude of silvers that shone in the moonlight, and when she moved her scales rasped together like a blacksmith's file shaping metal pieces. I could not see her face. I grabbed hold of my mother's hand and didn't let go until she made me get out of the carriage. My father led me to the dragon.

'Ailani, meet Pacu,' he said. The dragon bent her head down to me and looked me in the eye. And that's when I knew that my fears and dreams had all meant nothing and that I was going to be fine. I laughed.

'What's so funny?' my father asked.

'Pacu looks kind,' I said.

Pacu's face was somewhat horse-like. She had a long nose, elegantly curved, and enormous dark eyes. Her cheekbones were ridged with a hard cartilage that curled and swooped in a delicate filigree. There was a majestic crest that swooped from the middle of her head down her spine and somehow recalled a crown. She was more metal than flesh. She smiled at me and there was nothing frightening about her knife-like teeth. I was safe.

My father led me into the tower and made sure I was settled. As he turned to leave I asked him:

'What am I to do here?'

He took my hand and squeezed it.

'Dream of weddings,' he said. 'Talk of love.'

He left, locking the door behind him. I watched the carriage disappear from my bedroom window. And then I began my new life.

There is not a lot one can do in a tower in the middle of nowhere. But, one can read. The State had ensured that the tower was furnished with a multitude of books with which I could educate myself.

I read them all.

I learned a hint of state craft and a whisper of finance. I learned a smattering of philosophy and a smidgeon of history. I was blessed with a wealth of language books and

TIN GIRL

I learned everything about the history of art. I learned a lot
about kings. Many of their stories began with their quest to
save a princess from a dragon. Sometimes these princesses
were named. I read about weddings. I read about love.

What I could never find in any of these books was what
men would do when they weren't rescuing princesses, or
fighting wars, or ridding their lands of a general, somewhat
ill-defined evil. And as for the women, what did they do
when they weren't being rescued? Once I was out of my
tower what would my duties be? I would have a child of
course. Perhaps more than one. But what would I *do*? And
for that matter, what did other people do? The ones that
weren't royal or rich and important. What was it all for?

I asked Pacu a lot of these questions. She usually told me
she didn't know. Sometimes she would laugh but she would
never tell me what she found so funny.

'Pacu,' I said one day. 'How many princesses have you
guarded?'

Pacu raised her head and leant it on the enormous
windowsill so we could look at each other as we spoke.

'One,' she said. 'But I've been lucky. Dragons don't
usually survive a guarding.'

'So why do dragons do it?' I asked.

'The perks,' she said. 'A dragon has a big world to live in.
And when I die, the State will give my hatchling my weight
in treasure. And that's not including what my hatchling will
inherit from me.'

65

Pacu rose up on her legs then and bared her belly to me so I could see the gold and gems that were encrusted in her silver scales. They were a familiar sight but I had never thought of them as being part of an income before.

'I didn't know you had a hatchling,' I said.

'I don't!' Pacu told me. 'Not yet.'

I thought about that.

'If you don't survive this guarding you will never have a hatchling,' I said. It seemed a very sad thing to me. I would have liked to see another Pacu. But Pacu didn't seem sad at all. She smiled and said:

'Dragon hatchlings are made, not laid.'

'What does that mean?' I asked her.

She gave me an enigmatic wink, and that seemed the end of that conversation.

'So, what happened to the last princess you guarded?' I asked.

'She was never rescued.'

'Oh,' I said. Oh. Because there was nothing else to say. Pacu settled her head back on the window sill and looked at me. 'What was she like?' I asked her.

'She dreamed of weddings and spoke of love. She told me of her childhood sweetheart. He had promised he would find her and even though so many years had passed she still hoped that he would appear one day and rescue her.'

'He probably married someone else,' I said.

'Oh no!' Pacu told me. 'No. He applied to quest for her

every year but every year the State ruled that he wasn't a suitable match. Eventually, as the years kept passing, he decided to discard protocol and quest all the same. He found our tower and we talked. I had to tell him she had died a week before. He took that quite hard but we had a good conversation all the same.'

'What happened to him?'

Pacu cocked her head to one side – a dragon's version of a shrug.

'Did you like her? The other princess.'

'Well enough,' said Pacu.

'Did you like her as much as you like me?' I asked. I was smiling, only half serious, and Pacu laughed her grating metal laugh – razors on skin.

'She dreamed of weddings and spoke of love,' she said. I wasn't sure what she meant. She was quiet for a while and she surprised me when she spoke again. 'You, on the other hand,' she said. 'You seem like a tin girl.'

'What's a tin girl?' I asked.

Pacu gave me a long look. I felt weighed and measured.

'Are there no tin girls in your books?' she asked. I shook my head. 'Well then. Perhaps we shouldn't speak of them.'

* * *

I grew to love Pacu very quickly. It was hard, knowing that my freedom rested on her death, but when I mentioned it to her she would flaunt her belly and laugh. I understood that dragons don't think like humans.

The first suitor to make it to our tower didn't last very long. I was disappointed and relieved at the same time. Pacu didn't think much of him. The second suitor was just as bad. The third suitor had more luck.

I watched through the enormous window as they fought. Every time his sword clattered against her metal scales I jumped a little. I found myself willing Pacu to bite him clean in half but the man was so much faster than the others, always moving, always one step ahead of her. And then finally he had a chance and took it. Pacu reared up and came crashing down, intent on crushing him, but he stood in just the right spot, sword aimed for the only soft part of her flesh— a small patch of skin over her heart.

When Pacu died I was stunned.

I cried and didn't notice the man enter my room. I jumped when he touched my shoulder. He stepped away and let me grieve.

When the tears subsided my suitor offered me a rag, fairly dirty, but I took it and blew my nose in it all the same.

'So, you made it,' I said.

He sat down on my bed.

'I did,' he said and I could hear how exhausted he was. He lay back and stretched, and I thought: I wasn't expecting this. I had always thought that if Pacu was defeated I would be swept out of the tower immediately and taken back to the world I had left behind. I had never taken into account that fighting would be tiring and that a prince might have to rest. They never talked about that in the books.

'I was in two minds about applying for this,' the man said, not sitting up, just staring at the ceiling. I went to sit next to him. 'Six suitors had come back already, saying it was impossible. And the State told us that the other two were dead. It seemed like more trouble than it was worth.' He looked at me then. 'But you're pretty. That's good.'

I nodded.

'Yes. I am pretty,' I said. 'That part's not difficult.'

He sat up.

'What is difficult?'

'Being interesting.'

He nodded and smiled at me.

'Yes. That part's difficult. I haven't quite worked out how to do that myself.'

I almost wanted to laugh then. A dragon laugh, strange and grating.

'Come on,' he said, taking my hand and pulling me to my feet. 'It won't do for us to spend the night here alone. We have to go.'

I looked around.

'Who's going to know if we stay here?'

'The State knows everything,' he said, all too serious. So, I followed him. When we reached the tower door I hesitated. The sudden fear surprised me. After wanting to be outside for so long, I was now afraid of the world. He squeezed my hand.

'It'll be alright,' he said and by the way he said it, I knew he was right.

We stepped out into the late afternoon. Pacu's body glittered to one side. I looked at it once, said a silent farewell, and then followed this man away from the tower.

'What's your name?' I asked him.

'Bheka.'

'I'm Ailani.'

'I know.'

'Wasn't there an easier way for you to find someone to marry?' I asked him. He laughed.

'Plenty of easier ways,' he said. 'But it's family tradition to go questing, and I couldn't let them down. I thought about applying for a simpler quest; did you know there were four sphinxes I had to riddle away from on the way here? I thought about something simpler but...' he stopped then; both talking and walking.

'What?' I asked.

'I liked the sound of your name the best,' he said. He looked embarrassed and he shifted uncomfortably before walking briskly onwards.

I smiled to myself and whispered 'Ailani,' under my breath. That was my name. And he liked it.

'Of course, I can't take credit for my name,' I told him. 'I was given it.'

'I know. But I thought if your parents gave you such a beautiful name, they might be beautiful people too. And marriage doesn't just involve the two of us.'

This time I laughed. And then I was quiet, full of the world, soaking it all in: the smell of the dusk, the grass and the dust, the sound of the night birds waking. I looked around almost manically, not wanting to miss a detail. Bheka let me savour it all. He was quiet and considerate. I liked him.

The trip back to my kingdom was long and uneventful. Bheka told me the stories of what he did to find me. He told me of the roads he took and the people he met. Many were kind to him. They told him of the ones that had come through before. He told me of the sphinxes and the great marsh demon with the many heads. He told me of the fire swamp he had had to navigate. And then he told me of the fight with Pacu. She had looked him in the eye and laughed as he had walked up. So like Pacu to think that death was a joke.

But we met none of these things on the way back. Everything had vanished and the way was clear. I asked Bheka why this was so.

'The State sees to things like that!' he said, as if I should know all about it. I reminded him that I had been locked up in a tower since the age of twelve and knew little of the world outside of books. He took my hand.

'I'm sorry,' he said.

He told me of the world and things I didn't know. My State-approved books had failed to mention that the State was all and we were what we were because of it. It seemed that royals were less important than I had been led to believe. Of ordinary people, he could tell me very little.

He asked me about myself and I told him all I knew. I told him about Pacu too. I told him how sad I was that she would never have a hatchling. That the world seemed less bright without her big metal body sparkling in it.

When we reached my kingdom a celebration had already been prepared. I was amazed and said so.

'You shouldn't be,' said Bheka. 'The State provides.'

He led me up through the streets of the kingdom. The people formed lines about them and cheered as we passed. When we got to the castle it was just as I remembered it. My father, the king, stood on the stairs, and my lady mother stood just behind him, her head bowed, as if she wasn't ready to look at me. They behaved as if they had not seen me just last year on their visit to the tower. They embraced me and made much of me. They made even more of Bheka, and I heard the serving girls sigh as he walked past and whisper to each other about how handsome he was, and how brave and strong and clever. I knew they were right.

There was a feast and as the night drew closer to morning I was finally allowed to go back to my old room and rest. I went to the bed where I used to have such nightmares of my future, and lay down to sleep. I dreamt of the tower again, but this time it was not tall and frightening and I was not trapped in a room with a serpent. I woke up crying. I had left my home behind.

The next day, I was dressed and made up, just as I had been before. I was taken to my parents. Bheka was with them. And they, the three of them, took me to the State.

The State lived in a tower of its own. It was made up of twelve men and women, all imperious and imposing. When I looked from face to face I found I was afraid again. I rubbed my sweaty palms on the skirt of my dress and tried my best to look as serene as a princess should be.

'So,' said one man. 'Ailani. You have been rescued by a State-approved suitor. Custom decrees that you ask him to marry you.'

I was reminded of what Pacu had said of the princess she had guarded before. She dreamed of weddings and spoke of love. I had never dreamed of weddings nor spoken of love. I looked at Bheka. He was handsome, strong and brave. He had shown me he was kind, and he had shown us all that he was clever. He was a man that anyone would find easy to love. And yet I did not want to marry him.

'Well?' asked a woman of the state.

'Well?' I asked.

'Well, get on with it!' said another man of the state.

'Get on with what?'

'The proposal, girl! Get on with the proposal!'

'Ah. Right.' I looked at Bheka again. 'Bheka,' I said.

'Yes?' he asked, and he looked at me with such hope that I began to laugh. I laughed so hard I couldn't stop. Because it all seemed too absurd; from my cloistering all the way to Bheka's hopeful face when he didn't know me at all.

'What's she doing?' I heard one person of the State say to another.

'What's she doing?' I heard my father ask my mother.

'What are you doing?' I heard them all ask me. And then I heard myself say:

'I cannot marry him. I don't love him.'

I looked up at the State, all twelve of them, and they looked back at me, eyebrows raised.

'Well, this is really most irregular,' said one woman eventually. 'I suppose we can give her more time to get to know him?'

'More time?' said a man. 'Their journey back was strategically planned to give them all the time they needed. Bheka?' he said.

'Yes sir?' asked Bheka.

'Do you love Ailani?'

He looked at me shyly, before looking back at them.

'I believe I do. She's really quite a wonder.'

I blushed. It's always nice to hear someone thinks you're a wonder.

'You see,' said the man to the other members of the state. 'He's had enough time. Why should she need any more?'

'Well, not everyone is the same,' countered a woman.

'That's true,' the others agreed.

'How long do you think she might need?'

'Why don't we ask her?'

'Girl,' said a man. 'How long do you need to fall in love with... with... sorry,' he shuffled some papers on the table before him before giving up and asking Bheka: 'What's your name again?'

'Bheka,' said Bheka.

'Ah, yes. Sorry. We have several cases to get through today.' The man turned back to me.

'How long do you need to fall in love with Bheka?'

I thought about that before answering.

'I'm afraid I really don't know.'

The State muttered amongst themselves for some time before turning to me and saying:

'You have one month, and then you are to return here for a review.'

And that was it. We were hurried out and as we left I saw another princess beaming from ear to ear and holding tightly to her suitor's arm. I could imagine how their proceedings would go; she was practically proposing at the door.

'Right. Well. That was different,' said my mother.

Bheka took my hand.

'It's fine Ailani. We'll sort it all out in a month. I don't mind waiting.'

A month passed. My parents saw to it that I spent almost every waking hour with Bheka. He was charming, wonderful, incredibly talented. He taught me how to fish and how to juggle and how to throw knives. We spent evenings playing chess and talking about books. He made me laugh all the time and I found it more and more difficult to imagine any sort of future without him. So, when the month was over I was quite prepared to propose.

As before, the four of us went to the State. As before they asked me to propose. And as before, and quite to everyone's surprise, including mine, I said I couldn't. The State declared that another month would be given and they ushered us out quickly. Another couple passed us as we left and I saw another princess ready to ask the question I couldn't.

The month disappeared quickly. Bheka showed me his kingdom. He taught me how to read the stars, and how to track a falcon. I liked him very much.

I could not propose.

We were given another month.

Bheka gave me a treasure map and helped me find that treasure. He taught me to survive in the wild and he began to teach me the language of birds. I liked him more than anyone.

I could not propose.

The State was losing patience with our case. They gave us a year just to see the back of us for a while. We made the most of it, travelling across the continent, and setting sail for another. Bheka helped me pull a sea snake's tooth and together we captured a phoenix. He told me all the ways in which he loved me and he showed it too with his thoughtful manner, his quiet consideration. I couldn't bear the thought of losing him. I loved him.

But I could not propose. Because what would happen when I did? I had read enough stories. I knew what would be expected of me after our wedding.

This time the State had had enough.

'Enough!' yelled a man of the State. 'Enough, enough! I don't know about all of you, but I've had enough.'

The other members of State nodded their heads in vigorous agreement.

'The problem here isn't that this girl doesn't love...love... what's your name again?' he asked Bheka.

'Bheka,' Bheka said, so simply and so easily it made me want to laugh.

'Yes. Quite. Bheka. The problem isn't that she doesn't love Bheka, it's that she *can't* love. Not Bheka or anyone. The child is a *tin girl*.'

The whole room gasped at those words. The whole room but me. I just frowned. I remembered Pacu's words from so long ago. *Tin girl.*

'What's a tin girl?' I asked.

'He's saying you don't have a heart,' Bheka told me. I heard my mother begin to cry.

'But that's not right,' I argued. 'I do have a heart. I can love. How could I live if I didn't?'

'You don't have a heart and that's the end of it,' said the

State. 'You are a TIN GIRL!'

There was something frightening about those words. I began to panic.

'But what does that mean?' I asked. 'What happens now?'

'What happens now?' said the State. 'What happens now is that you go back to your tower. Only this time you won't be living in it. You will be guarding it.'

My heart stopped for a moment. A long moment. Such a long moment that I suddenly feared they were right and that I didn't have a heart. But then it started beating so hard I thought it might burst from my chest.

'No,' I said. 'No! Why?'

'Well we can't have tin girls running around freely,' said a woman of the State. 'That could cause chaos. It's quite catching, tin girlishness. I only wish we'd noticed sooner; who knows how many people you might have ruined with your reckless thoughts.'

And my reckless thoughts began to whirl with all the things I had done since I had left my tower, all the adventures I'd had. My world had got so big and now they wanted to take it all away from me again. All because I would not marry and live in a shrunken world.

'But what harm am I doing?' I asked. My voice was so small and frightened.

'What harm? What harm?' The State began to laugh, all twelve of them, terrible, nervous laughs and I could see that they were afraid of me. I turned to my father.

'Please. Please don't let them do this,' I asked of him. He shook his head.

'What can I do? I'm only a king.'

'Mother!' I cried. 'Mother you can't let them do this to me!' My mother only cried.

'Bheka!' I pleaded. 'Help me.' He just looked at me helplessly and held up his hands.

'Tin girls are dangerous,' he said.

'You shall be given an income,' a man of the State said. 'And we will assign you an inheritance. Let's say... the dragon Pacu's hoard hasn't been claimed. She can have that one, can't she?' he asked the others. They all nodded in agreement. Pacu's hoard? But it was for her hatchling. I was not her hatchling! I remembered her words: *Dragon hatchlings are made, not laid.*

'Why?' I shouted. 'Why are you so afraid of me?' I asked the State. They looked at me very seriously.

'Because all girls must dream of weddings and talk of love.'

"My wife and I often go canoe-ing on the Cam from Cambridge to Grantchester, and many a story can be dreamed up on this river with the punting accidents and wild swim-ming abound. I have an affinity with mermaids and I found Una on one trip. She wouldn't let me go until I'd told her story."

ALEXA RADCLIFFE-HART
www.servicestoliterature.co.uk

Alexa is a writer of short tales, the more obscure the better, but always with a big heart and often a history of stories behind it. She's currently writ-ing a novel (again), is in a long term relationship with Writers' HQ, and is marketing bod for hire.

River Girls

THE GIRL'S FIRM STANCE alters slightly as I appear next to her on the water's edge. Her mother is already reclined in the punt with a new born, her son, suckling. Her father, attempting to balance in the hull, notices me as the girl does, from the feet up. I tower above them both but his fear leaks from his pores rather than his face. The girl changes the unknown into curiosity. They always do.

"Who are you?"

I bend to conspire at her height.

"I am a river girl. You can call me Bridget. Why don't you like the water?"

"She's scared of the boat. Come on, Lucy. There's nothing to be afraid of. I used to take your Mummy out on these all the time when we were younger."

The metal pole spears the water at an odd angle, the punt swaying as he tries again to offer her a hand. The girl turns to face me again.

"Lucy, are you afraid of the water or the boat?" She wrinkles her nose in reply but her blue eyes meet mine.

"We could give you one of these..."

I show her the tiny life jacket worn by a hundred other scared, excited, uncontrollable children.

"... although the mermaid would always save you."

A smile creeps into her eyes, astonishment adorning her lips.

"Mermaid? Here?"

Her father's sigh interrupts us.

"Oh, you'll never get rid of her now."

"Would you like me to tell you about her?"

"Yes! Yes!"

"Well, mermaid stories can only be told on boats, on water. Shall we go for a punt?"

"I couldn't possibly... You must have customers who have paid for a tour..."

His protests falter as I extend my hand towards the pole. He relinquishes it until it stands awaiting my next command. The boat sways as he settles next to his brown eyed family.

My bare feet flatly balance on the till and the girl lifts her arms ready to be held. Her sides are small in my grasp, fingers reaching around her back as I swing her from the land into the blanketed hull. She sits comfortably, they all do, as I push us away from the mooring.

"There is a mermaid who watches over this river, but she isn't like the stories you've been told before."

* * *

Una's shoulders roll forwards, swooping her arms through the water. As she slows, her head bobs above. She knew where she would be but seeing it is different to feeling the temperature change at the point where the currents collide. On the surface, at the bend in the river, the only sign is the ripples that beach against her neck. The nettles wave to her from the bank and leaf boats float past, racing each other in teams of colour. She continues, thinking only of the gasp of breath between strokes. As she nears the shallows of her section of the river, the cool shadow of the trees becomes confused with a memory, so she has to surface. She expects to see his feet, a sign he would join her in her river play, but of course they are not there. Only an empty wheelchair waits for her.

* * *

"Once there was a girl who could swim. Her mother felt her swimming in the bubbling tide within her which grew to strokes and flicks as her belly stretched to keep her inside as long as possible. Her mother had strong land-locked feet that held the weight of them both for over half a year. When the girl swam out, her cries brought joy. Too soon they were replaced by the umm and ahh of people who should have warned her mother. The girl had surfaced in the wrong world."

* * *

"What's her name, Bridget? How old is she? How far can she swim in a day? Are there more of her, more mermaids, here? Why does she live in the river, not the sea? What is her bed like? Does she sleep in the water? What does she dream of? What does she eat? How fast can she swim? How long will she live? What colour is her tail? How does she breathe? Where does she go on holiday?"

* * *

"The girl began her life in a place without water. There were many suggestions made by doctors, well-wishers, those who wanted the girl to be like them. When they were sure that she would live in this world, they named her Una. The only time Una seemed not to struggle was in the bath. At first, she was cradled by her father's hands but soon, her arms and hips grew strong. Her father knew that they had to find a new home, to be near the water.

The house he found was perfect. The inside was beautiful enough for the mother and had a large sloping garden surrounded by tall fences and at the bottom, a wide hedge which hid the closeness of the river from view. All the privacy and freedom they needed.

Una's father built a jetty, strong enough to hold them both, connecting the bank to the water. At first he would carry her out but later she used the wheelchair that moved her around in their world. The greatest joy was to hear her laughter in and out of the water."

* * *

"Una swam away to the sea. Her parents slipped onto another life. In the remembering of the past, she swam with the tales her father told each bedtime, tales full of merfolk, sea monsters and heroines, older stories with sacrifices for a new life and love. The fantasies left questions that she was unable to ask now. Why would someone who could live in a world of water trade their voice, their freedom, their beautiful scales for a life on land? Love cannot be that strong surely? Could she find a sea-witch to help her? But for and what would she trade?

Now a woman, she pushed past the boundaries of her home previously set within a half-day swim so she could return as she should, as she had been told. The river told her of the pull of the sea, the currents leading her body when she grew tired, allowing her to float with the sun's warmth on her face. She followed the course of untamed rivers, their mouths leading into one another. The sounds below the water mainly stayed the same, there was comfort in that. Above the flow, bird sounds changed as often as the scenery, the land getting flatter every time she surfaced. Soon, the taste of salt laced her lips."

* * *

"Who are you?" Una's lips crack as the words escape towards the woman holding her. Una had ignored the river's warnings and lies beached by the low tide. The Wash whispers its promises with the slap of every wave as it creeps back.

"A river girl. Call me Bridget. Would you like some help?"

Una accepts the binding of a blanket, the rough wool held tight by Bridget's arms as she pulls her up to sit, her legs limp in the mud.

"I need to find a sea-witch."

"What would you want one of those for?" Bridget's face is hidden in their embrace, still Una can hear her disgust. Una tries to make her voice stronger but the lack of use keeps her quiet.

"I want to be a mermaid. The tide will take me where I need to be. I am waiting."

"The tide does not hold all the answers. I have watched you swim, listen to the river chatter, use its will to find a way. You are already what you seek."

"I want to be free. I need a tail."

"Fins don't mean freedom. Do you understand what you would have to give? Not just give, but sacrifice?"

"I don't have anything left."

"What about the river? It has been part of your home – the sea-witch would want to take that. She would love to fill

86

the rivers, push herself onto the land."

"I don't care for the land. She can have it."

"You don't care for the world that saved you? The barriers you can cross on land would give you access to so many other places, so many other rivers. Our fresh waters heal and can abate any thirst."

"Rivers and land have confined me. The sea offers true freedom."

"True, the depths you would have are unparalleled, but you would sacrifice sun and air as well as land – unable to surface you would be kept under the sea."

"But..." Thoughts slow Una's tongue. "But I would have friends there."

"Do you already know mermaids?"

"No, but they would be my people."

"Would they? The mermaids you know are of stories, reality can be different."

Una slumped back into Bridget's arms, her warmth kinder than the wind buffering them with salt spray from the shallow pools.

"I have always wanted a tail."

"You can have a tail. Look."

Her splayed limbs, blue and purple from her journey and the chill of the sea air, silvered with scales, her feet spread into a fin under a layer of mud. Una blinks and her lifeless legs return.

"But with it you would be trapped in the water. As you

are, you have access to all the freedom you need. You can be both."

* * *

Finding a place to turn the boat around was easy once the learners, the show-offs, the drifters were clear of us.

Lucy continued to listen whilst my words wove a sleep that cradled her parents and brother. Later the father would place paper that meant nothing in my hands, with thanks that came from his eyes, from his wife's relaxed limbs, from his calm son, from the kiss goodbye from Lucy which would mean everything.

But before that, Lucy and I carried on with the story until we reached the shallows. Before we drifted into the shade of the willows and thirsty birch, Lucy pointed at the bank. Her fingers joined the pointed forefinger until her hand relaxed. She waved to the empty greying wheelchair on the slick green jetty, before looking back to me.

"Where's Una?"

"This story is for all the strong women of colour that have been forgotten. It's not enough, but I hope it's a start."

AMIRAH MOHIDDIN

Instagram @eternally_bookish

After losing her Harry Potter inspired 80,000 word novel at 11, Amirah swore never to return to writing. Until she did. Now that's she's back, she can't let go. A whimsical daydreamer, dangerously addicted to writing, Amirah loves writing dark fantasy stories full of adventure. She specialises on feminist retellings of fairy tales, drawing inspiration from strong women in Islamic history and literature.

I'll Show You a Villain

"YOU WANT A VILLAIN?" I drawl. "I'll show you a villain."

A breeze filled with the scent of smoke and the trill of screams rushes in from the window I climb through. They bring a slight flush to my cheeks, one that my victim can't see because of the mixture of the cool air and my own fires, bending light at will. With one hand I adjust the swan-shaped paperweight in front of me, with the other, I tighten my clutch on the throat of the owner of this grand house. I can see the red veins of his eyes imploring me to let him go.

I snort. "No offence, this is just business. I've got to make a living somehow."

He nods profusely as though he understands my whole life story. I lean down and chuckle in his ear. "Still, no one ever said I was nice."

He shudders. I lurch back before any of his stuffy breath hits me. As I do, I feel one of my earrings tangle with the fabric of my hijab.

I loosen my grip on him, but don't let go completely. Instead, I use my other hand to remove my sunshine earrings from the fabric. "I'm not holding that tight. After all, I don't want you to die."

No, I just want him to suffer enough that he'll do what I want. I wag a finger at the million riya pen and beckon it towards me. The man croaks as he draws in air. His eyes dart to the side and he pushes against my hand.

His arms jerk towards the table before I have a chance to stop him. I burn the legs of his chair with a thought and knock him down with one swift motion. He drops onto the ground in a thud. I raise my leg and bring my booted foot down where my hand once was. Not hard enough to kill him, but enough that it hurts.

"Tut tut," I say, crouching down to see what he was aiming for. There's a button on the underside of the table. "Do you honestly think anyone will come to help you?" I jerk my head towards the door where smoke creeps through the crevice at the bottom. "Why do you think I set fire to your house?"

He whimpers.

"Oh, for fun?" I tilt my head. "Yes, that too."

I take away my heel and use the toe of my boot to wipe the man's tears. Removing my foot, I grab him by the collar and push him against his own desk.

"Tell me where it is," I snarl.

"I don't know," he cries.

"Do better."

"I... in the bathhouse. It's in the bathhouse," he says. But I can smell the lies in his breath.

"You know I'm a jinn? I can tell when you're lying." I gesture at the smoke. "And you're lying."

He begins to sob. I press harder.

"It's in the library," he shouts. "In the park!"

I grab the pen and smack into the desk where a scrap of paper lies under the man's drool.

"Draw a map," I order.

I look around the room, outside the window. As I expected no one has come around to this side of the house. I stuff the piece of paper into the pocket of my jeans as soon as he's done, cringing at the wetness.

When I let go, he begins to scream. "Help! Help!"

"Where's the trust? I thought we had a good thing going," I say. He glances at me and then the door. I pause for good measure. "No one's coming."

He slides off the edge of the table, slumping to the ground. One hand still grips onto it as his eyes search his whole history.

I climb out back out of the window, propping my feet onto the stone ground outside. "You should've been nicer to them," I say finally.

I take care when I get out, one hand on my hijab and the other bunching up the floor-length robe I wear. The man I'm leaving behind manages to press the emergency button and the security alarm raves loudly in my ear. I steady myself and flitter in and out of visibility as I exit the property through the hulking large gates and find my way to the park.

Even ten minutes away, in the park next to the property, I can smell the smoke that's turning to soot.

"Naar," I whisper. I feel the force I released on the house return to its rightful place beneath my skin. The darkness absorbs the warmth of the sun. The heat gives me life.

When I enter the woods, songbirds sing and the bells of bicycles ring. I reach the path of an old library. I drag my feet, wiping the mud caught on my heels on the cobblestones that lead to the protruding porch. Paper birds flutter overhead, seeming to urge me forward and keep me away.

A flitter of fire runs through my veins. I want to find the book first. A thrill travels up my spine, as though leeching the heat from me.

Entering the library, I am met by a staircase. It gives me a homely feeling, but not from nostalgia or personal experience. It reminds me of what people in school have said that home feels like, comfy, familiar and safe. I wouldn't know.

The handrails of the staircase arch in pleasure, the steps creaking and moaning as I travel up. There are chips missing in the wood, and rough carvings as though someone tried to write Welcome, but didn't have enough time to finish. 'Welco' it greets.

As I go up, the steps seem to light up. Paper lanterns float above the handrails, guiding me forward. I continue to ascend, gaping in awe at the lines of shelves revealing themselves to be a domino trail across the first floor. The redwood floors creak as I leave each step behind, an echo of my haunting. The steps diverge, giving me two paths but only one continues to be lit.

The steps dim as I reach the third floor. I step onto a platform, walking past a window that is the only indicator of time. I snort bitterly. Because I am a Jinn, people think me timeless. But I'm not exempt. Time is not merciful, it is heartless and cruel. Some say it is indifferent, but that's not true. When you're immortal, time exists, in the manner of a noose around your neck and an audience that thrives on the tension, waiting, before the panel beneath your feet opens up.

I slip into one of the aisles, the shelves densely packed with books. Folklore, myths and curses. Light sparks from my fingertips, catching the scent of stale coffee. It's almost intoxicating. I wonder if the staircase knew to bring me here. I sweep my fingertips across the spines, skimming over the titles. All the stories of my kind tormenting and gifting mortals. It's not what I'm looking for, not what I'm in the mood for. It's my avarice, I want to be more than just a side character for the humans.

Finally, my mind hones in on a book with a blank spine. This one feels different. I free it from its cage and flip it around. There's nothing on the back either.

This is the book. I can feel it in every ember of fire in my bones. I pull it from its place and flick the pages open.

My shoulders fall, the pages are blank. For something so notorious, there's nothing to it. It's held together by string rather than glue or magic.

I pause for a moment and scan the shelves around me. None of the books even try to take any space in my mind. And my mind doesn't let any of them in. Looking back down at the book, I wonder if it's the right one, or if my instinct has wavered.

No. It's never done that. This is the book. I'm sure of it. But I can't sell it without any proof that it works.

I inspect it further. The cover is a rich burgundy, striking to the eye. The title has faded. Written in gold plating, it had either been rubbed off or had disappeared with time, leaving it a husk of its former glory. The pages feel ragged under my touch.

I flip it open again. The pages are still unmarked. There's no story, no words.

"Ayqizh," *awaken*, I say to the book, rapping my index and middle finger on the cover.

Nothings happens.

I consider shelving it, but my hands begin to tremble. Another dead end, another day completely wasted. Disappointment sinks within me like molten lead, destroying everything in its path. Another hope dashed.

I begin to shake, afraid of the fall from my soaring hope. This has happened before, I remind myself. This isn't the first time. This is just another day. I just have to try again.

But when I reach into myself to try and smother my fires, I realise that I'm not the one who's upset. I'm not trembling or shaking. The book is.

Reflex loosens my grip on it, but I clutch back down. A shock runs through me and I'm forced to drop the book to the ground.

"Pesky magic," I seethe.

The book opens, ink droplets forming and seeping onto the blank page. I hold my breath.

The ink has begun to take shape, forming into links of a chain. Below words begin to form.

The girl opened the book.

In there she found blank pages.

The story began to write itself.

She is at the beginning of her story,

And at the end.

The book begins to shudder on the floor, writhing. It begins to emit a blue light. I feel my fires swell inside me with the first hint of panic and I edge along the aisle. I can feel the cold rush of air as the magic from the book edges towards me. I try to push it back with all my might.

"Dar'a," *shield*, I say.

But the magic continues. I bump into the shelf and stop short. I thrust myself past others and dash to the end of the aisle. And when I get there, I run past more. I need to get out.

Thump, thump.

My heart catches in my throat at the sound. I glance over my shoulder, but the sound continues. It's not coming from behind me. I turn around and see the window. The paper birds knock, the creatures slowing me down as they throw themselves against the glass over and over. Where they were white before, one now has a blackened wing and the other a scrawled-upon head. It has the gall to look me dead in the eye and gesture to the lock on the window.

"I'm in the middle of a chase," I hiss the last word as though I haven't paused long enough.

Their energetic fluttering stops. They freeze. So do I. A cold creeping sensation crawls up the side of my leg. I look down to see my boots coated with wet ink and spiralling around my leg. It inches closer to my hip and thighs. My heart stops, my shoulders tense.

I'm jolted off my feet, legs first, my body plunging in the air as a hindsight. Dragged backwards, I claw against the redwood floorboards. I send flickers of fire, but they only leave burn marks on the floor. Everything vanishes except the large closing pages above me like an apocalyptic sky.

And then it reappears again. Only, this time I'm on my knees with a chain around my neck and cuffs on both of my wrists. I kneel before a platform, on which a throne and a husky sit in anticipation. The platform is made of marble, with a lace pattern adorning its surface. The steps around the platform look as delicate as candy petals artfully placed to make the platform look like it's hovering.

The chains I wear have subdued my power so that there are only whispers of it left. There are a dozen people looking at me, lined up around huge portraits of monarchs, framed in gold and guarded by large velvet drapes and actual soldiers. My skin crawls as they catch me watching, a goose bump rising for every pair of eyes. But the one that makes mine widen is the one sitting on that red-gold throne. She sits next to the husky, stroking its fur with her pink tipped nails. We are opposites. Her hair is as blonde as mine is black and her skin so pale that I doubt she'd spent a moment in the sun.

Two facts flash into my mind. The first is that I'm inside the book, and the second, the woman on the throne is the queen.

"That throne is mine," I say. The words come out of my mouth faster than I can stop them.

I blink, shock ricocheting in my chest. A swear bubbles on my lips but it doesn't enter the atmosphere. I'm beginning to realise why I'm in these chains.

I tug on my earlobe, sandwiching it between the fabric of my hijab, pinching it between my finger and thumb and yanking it repeatedly. Magical though I am, even I have to check whether this is a dream or not. It decidedly is not. I tilt my head and grin, and then when I hear the gasps around me, I lap them up.

I'm blinded by how much treasure there is in this room. I roll my eyes. They burn as I do. I raise my hand and jangle my chains.

"What charge am I being held on?"

The queen glares at me. I guess that means I'm not allowed to ask questions. It may also mean that the queen herself wanted to ask the very same question.

"Sannan," she says, flicking her wrist.

A wolf pads towards the queen. Yes, a wolf, I'm not hallucinating that large white furred animal with beady silver eyes. As it walks, a wind seems to ripple across its fur blowing into a human shape. I've never seen a shifter change in front of me before, it's like watching someone undress. Am I supposed to look away?

From the wake of the animal, a man wearing a fitted batik shirt with a blue lattice strides towards her. He looks at me his grin wolfish and his eyes narrowed.

"Well she certainly doesn't look like a villainess," he says.

The queen laughs, it sounds like tinkling bells. I bet she snorts like a pig in private. "That headwrap of hers makes her look more hostile to me."

Okay, rude.

Sannan lifts his head and looks up at the ceiling as though he's thinking. "She reminds me more of a doll my mother used to give me."

My nostrils flare as I draw in a deep breath, the depths of my lungs aching with the compression. "I suppose you used that doll as a chew toy, mutt?" I snap.

All eyes in the room turn to me. Sannan's widen and his

lips stretch into a cruel upturned smile.

"Rest assured, I've had practice, so I won't be kind." As he speaks his voice lowers. I meet his gaze, anger fizzing in me, blowing bubbles of excitement.

The queen snaps her fingers behind him.

"Patience, woman," I say, glaring at her. "We were having a moment there."

Her lips purse. As though that's signal enough, a guard takes the chain from the queens hands and yanks it forward. I gag, thrown to the queen's feet. I cough and splutter and choke out my tongue.

"You should really learn to be more careful," I say. "A dead villainess is no villainess for the people. And no villainess means no one to blame."

The queen looks at me as though I'm dirt under her toes.

"Her crimes," she repeats, her voice leaden.

I've decided. She's not fun, and if she's not fun, then I don't like her. The wolf-boy on the other hand is nice to look at and I could listen to him talk all day.

"The prisoner has committed numerous crimes against the crown. She has murdered officials, stolen magic, mutilated and mutated creatures, destroyed property and shown no remorse for any of her crimes."

"How do you plead?" the queen asks.

I scoff and roll my eyes to the high heavens.

"Clearly not repentant, Sannan," she says.

I laugh. A hearty laugh, because this scene is incredulous.

I push against the steps and spit on the shoes with their toes curling upwards. I glare at the queen as Sannan takes my reigns and drags me away from her. He forces me back to my knees.

"Apologise," Sannan barks.

There's no way. It's time for me to play my role.

"No," I say. I place my hand on the floor and the chains linking them jangle. "You want a villain?" I say. "I'll show you a villain." I click my fingers and snarl, "Naar."

Fire rains down into the throne room, whipped around by air.

* * *

Like a phoenix, I rise and peer into the darkness around me. The gold has been left charred. The back of my throat closes as I look to the bodies strewn on the ground. My body convulses and the chains that bind me clink. I heave onto the floor as my knees buckle and give way to my tired weight.

The pages of the book flutter above my head and I feel the drag of the magic on my skin. The book wanted a villain and that's exactly what I gave it. Now the story is over, I'm dragged through the paper, back into the library. I hurriedly flip through the manuscript to the last page. Its final words read:

Sometimes, the villain wins.

"Romances in Greek mythology are, typi-cally, ill-fated. I wrote how to love a mor-tal as a cathartic rally-cry against the usual outcomes, creating something that may not have a happy ending, but does have a happy middle."

CHLOE DYSON-ASHER
Twitter @chloesmusings

Chloe never sets out to write anything sad, but she's influenced by Greek mythology and the two seem to go hand-in-hand. If she's not writing, she'll be attempting to hold court with castle ghosts – it never works, but it makes for great storytelling.

How to Love
a Mortal

I

IT STARTS, AS MOST THINGS concerning mortals do, with a word: don't.

Your sister whispers it when she notices the way your gaze catches on the young man across the room. He's alone, hair in his eyes, as he sits bent over a sketchbook.

Your sister's nails hook into your arm sharply enough that welts of gold pool in the wounds.

'You were not born to love,' she hisses, low and dangerous. Coffee spills across the table where her elbow knocked the cup. '*Stay away*. He will die; you will live.'

You know she means well. She's listing names, using them as warnings. The problem is you've never been good at heeding warnings.

II

Stay away.

You don't.

If he asked, you wouldn't tell him that spilling your coffee over his shirt was deliberate; you'd merely say it was a chance introduction. An introduction which turns into a date, which turns into two, three, four.

On the fifth, he asks if he can paint you. Over the millennia, artists and sculptors have whitewashed you, carved you in the image of a warrior victorious in combat. He paints you soft, dark skin bathed in the golden hour.

It is the only painting that matters.

Your sister still doesn't approve, and she probably never will. She cannot, however deny the way you're smiling more; it's been too long since you did.

He kisses you first, and it's raining and terribly cliché and perfect. You were not made to love, but you kiss him back anyway. You kiss him because he is temporary, you are not, and what harm can a kiss possibly do?

III

You are a liar and a thief. But he has settled into your soul, and you cannot stop the truth from tumbling from your lips. He does not believe you to be a god.

Why would he? Your life is subject to the testimony of

believers and, over the last few decades, you'd begun to feel more like a ghost. The only way you know how to make a mortal believe you is to spill the ichor in your veins. You heal in less than a second.

He does not run. He looks at you, and smiles, and tells you that he will take you – always – as you are.

You've spent so many centuries with a hollow space where your heart once was. But here is a boy who's crawled into your heart and patched up the walls.

You've never felt more solid than when you sleep with his arms around you.

IV

It is odd, isn't it? The way your hands tremble as they wander and explore the map that is his skin. Here, the constellations aligned in his freckles. Here, his ribs like the columns of a temple.

When he whispers that he trusts you, the words echo like a prayer in your head. You're the deity, but when you press your lips to the hollow of his throat his name in your mouth sounds like worship.

Making love to him feels like placing down the foundations of a home, doesn't it?

V

Even if you wanted to, you couldn't walk away if you tried.

VI

It happens in the small hours.

You are of the sun but these moments, when you're staring up at the morphing shadows spread across the ceiling, and he's dreaming beside you, have you praying for dawn to never break.

Dawn means a new day, him a day older. You are an ageless god.

The simple truth is that you've spent so long removing yourself from the battles of men that defence has become an alien concept. You are without shield, without armour. It feels like a blow, or the fatal blade of a sword to the stomach, the dawning realisation that there will be no one else after him.

How can there be? *He is it.*

This is why gods are not made to love mortals.

How are you going to survive this?

VII

His hair starts to grey at the temples. It was inevitable.

For so long you'd forgotten he was mortal. You think, maybe, he forgot too.

When you're outside, he begins to widen the distance

between the two of you; the inch of space between your hand and his has become no-man's land. Even in the safety of your apartment, he's occasionally turning away.

You're the one with a thousand statues carved in your image, but some nights it feels as though there is marble in your bed.

The mirror has turned into a wall and the time between his smiles has grown larger.

He confesses: the lines beside his eyes, around his mouth, make him self-conscious. You say you've never seen anything as beautiful.

You don't say you worry about the day you'll forget the sound of his laugh.

VIII

Sometimes you think that you should let him go.

Your sister had been right.

He will die.

You're sat in her apartment, holding a bow you haven't held in centuries, when you break down for the first time. The wood is as gnarled as the callouses on his knuckles.

You should have listened to her warnings. You should have stayed away.

You should have kept to the nature of a god, never remade yourself to love a mortal.

'Oh, brother,' your sister says. Her voice is soft.

You would rather meet her bite and steeled eyes.

'Look at the life you have built.'

She raises your left hand; the gold band on your forth finger glistens as it catches the sunlight.

'He chose you, chose this, and knew from the start how this would end.'

Gods shouldn't love, but you're a selfish creature in love with heartbreak.

IX

You want to scatter him across the stars or make a flower from his blood. But you no longer know how.

Is this how Achilles felt when you played a hand in the murder of Patroclus?

X

He dies. You endure.

"I wanted to write a magical-realist account of the feeling of alienation – not-at-homeness – that comes with an unhappy mental state. I also invoke the Welsh notion of 'Hiraeth', which describes a longing for a home from which one is estranged – a forgotten, imagined or half-remembered home, or a home that cannot be returned to – accompanied by a sense of estrangement and incompleteness."

REBECCA IRVIN

Rebecca Irvin is a writer currently living and working as an arts journalist in London. Her writing meditates on human relationships and is influenced by fiction which renders reality via the symbolic and the mystical – for example, the writings of Toni Morrison and Anne Michaels.

The Opposite of Home

AS SOON AS I LEARNED TO SPEAK, I began to recount the life
I had before this one, the life I had beneath the sea. My
half-articulated, childish sentences were full of flickering,
shimmering things, fins and scales, strung together like
pearls. When I started to walk, I asked my mother if we
wore shoes to anchor our feet to the ground and stop us
from floating away and bobbing up at the surface like silvery
pockets of air. I asked because my own grip on the earth
felt so precarious. I spoke of being cradled and rocked by a
watery tide, of tiny iridescent fish darting between my fingers
and toes, of eels encircling my waist with their rubbery
bodies. As I grew, I pieced together my broken memories
of that world like fragments of shell, held each one close,
a glittering treasure. I yearned for my ocean companions,
seals who nuzzled at my chin with whiskery faces, laughing
dolphins with velvet skin, great whales whose sonorous
voices enveloped me in their deep indigo song and tugged
at my heart from across vast wastes of ocean, sea nymphs
who braided my hair into long, thick ropes intertwined with
slippery cords of seaweed, who decorated my brow with a

crown of bleached white coral, who slid rings of mother-of-pearl onto every one of my fingers, whose hands and feet were webbed and whose eyes were shiny flattened discs like those of a fish.

I drew myself as an outline in coloured pencil and I filled it in with dark blue.

I was torn from my ocean home, rolled over and over in the waves, plucked from the cool quiet gloom like a blind crab from beneath a rock. I tumbled, gasping, into this loud world, helpless and naked as an oyster, shell prised open to expose pink, buttery flesh. Here, colours scream at me and sounds lash out like the arms of a jellyfish and leave me with angry welts. This world is red and swollen, filled with warm bodies pushing up against one another. Too close, and too bright. Each thing seen so exactly and with such painful clarity.

Blood, once blue, is pumped from the body scarlet and burning. Startlingly, staggeringly red.

My vacant face. My wide, staring eyes. I made other children nervous. I could see their lips tremble and their fingers twitch when they looked at me before looking quickly away again when I noticed them staring. They avoided my gaze as though afraid they might be sucked in to drown in the unblinking blue-black, deep and gaping as a ravine that splits open the seabed.

I became older and my limbs unfurled. My arms and legs became long and thin. Blue veins fanned out beneath the skin at my chest and wrists. Nobody called me beautiful. The word they used was *striking*, which always sounded like an accusation, like I was something that it hurt to look at. I could never work out exactly how and where I fit into the noisy, messy lives of those around me. I existed on the other side of a pane of glass behind which I could retreat into a calm and silent world where piercing voices could not reach me.

I had lovers. Purely out of curiosity. I was looking for something in each of them, something I could not name precisely, but which I could sometimes taste in the corners of their mouths and in the sweat that poured from their bodies.

I filled my mouth with it. I used my tongue to explore the folds in their skin and unearthed little crystals of salt, buried like precious gems.

Theirs was earth-salt, gritty and sandy in my mouth like licking a stone, the smell dark and coarse in my nostrils and not at all like the clean turquoise sea-tang that washed over me in my dreams.

The receptors for tasting salt are located on either side of the tongue. Sweet is at the tip. Sour is somewhere in the middle. Bitter is right at the back, just before you swallow. I think that my tongue is particularly receptive to salt. I can even taste it on the underside.

My lovers' bodies shivered when I touched them. *Bad circulation* they would tell me and then would blow hot breath into my cupped hands where it pooled, hot and sticky like warmed-up milk. They laughed at me when I twisted my fingers into their damp hair to imagine myself tangled up in strands of seaweed and kelp. They found it endearing when I brought my ear close to their lips so that their murmurs would sound like waves whispering through a seashell. And they cried when I told them I had to leave them because I could no longer bear their scorching hands and their rough skin and their heaviness.

The chest-crushing weight of them.

This one here, now, sleeps beside me like a child. I call him *husband*, which means *master of the house, house* which means *our house, house* which says *home* but means *not-home*. He is softer and gentler than the others. His fingernails are small and brown like the shelled skins of some sweet nut. A hazelnut. Or an almond. His wrists are delicate and where they are joined to his hands the bones jut out under the skin. He has light bones, like a bird's, they might be entirely hollow, I am not sure, but I would believe it if I was told it. Yes, if someone told me that I am sure I would not think it untrue. His voice is like new leaves. He had been lost, like me, and when he came upon me he held out his hand, shyly, palm open and flat, facing up, the way you would approach a frightened animal, and I climbed into it and curled up like a shell and he carried me away from the noise and the heat and the gaping faces and he set me down in this sleepy coastal town which is hewn out of grey rock and spattered with salt and guano, where days drift in and out with the breeze and when evening comes shadows stretch long tapering fingers over wet sand.

I could almost have loved him. It is almost enough. This calm, this quiet, and the coolness of his arms. But he is too much of the earth, eyes full of oak and flint and hair like damp peat. Neither of us is able to give the other what it is that we are searching for. For the most part, we are just companionable, I in my silence and he in his. I let him fill the bathtub and sinks with clods of soil and leafy green plants and he lets me paint rippling blue lines on all the walls.

I spend my days sketching the outlines of thorny stars, collecting shells and stones and pieces of smooth coloured glass which I thread onto lengths of twine and hang in clusters in every room. Each morning I rise early and walk barefoot on the beach that is exactly nine steps from the back door of this house. I seldom meet other people and when I do they avert their eyes and I stare at my toes. The ocean seethes at my feet and whips my ankles. I do not think that it recognises me. At night, I lie awake and listen to it breathing in and out. Lull-a-by. When I float weightless into black sleep, other sounds come to me in the dark, faint and far away, from beneath the skin of a silent sea. I hear the lowing calls of whales, the trickling fizz of bubbles. It is a language I have forgotten how to speak. No longer a part of that world nor fully in this one, I am in vertigo, teetering on the edge of a precipice. I am afraid of falling and at the same time I am terrified that if I stay still too long the bones in my shins will turn to stone and crumble away.

My stomach is filled with blue and it gets bluer every day.

The bluer it gets the more I'm sure the blue won't go away.

There are no stars tonight, but the moon is fat and it leans heavily on the horizon. I know that this will be one of those nights when I do not sleep, when I am pulled up like a drowning sailor every time I am about to sink and slip into the dark. I am too hot under this clinging sheet. I pull it off.

I stare up at the ceiling where there is a stripe of moonlight, clean and sharp as a knife. The window is open and I am not wearing anything because the clothes get twisted up in the sheets. The night air feels good on my skin. I am thirsty.

I swing my legs over the side of the bed and press the soles of my feet against the wooden floor to assure myself of its solidity. He breathes silently beside me. He is asleep. The house is quiet.

Beyond its walls, I hear the water thrumming like a heartbeat, keeping pace with my own pulse. I can feel it throbbing gently at the base of my spine and between my eyes. I stand up and, without putting anything on, pad downstairs to the kitchen.

Everything is bathed in the same blue hue. The shiny stack of saucepans next to the sink. The spilled oil on the counter. The bowl full of fresh plums which look like bruises. The jug of milk which has been left out next to the fridge. I look down at my body and it too is blue. A beautiful, deep blue. I do not go to the tap to get a drink.

Instead I take the key to the back door from beneath the bowl of plums and quietly let myself out onto the stone path that leads from the house to the beach. One two three four five six seven eight nine.

On my way I drop the key and it falls with a dull thud into the wet earth. I hardly realise I have done it and I do not stop to pick it up. Such a petty thing, I think, a key. Like a bottle cap or a tea strainer. Something that inserts itself insolently between you and what you are doing. It is like that with most things, I think. Yes, now that I think about it.

The marram grass at the top of the beach brushes against my legs as I step onto the sand. The sand is blue too, and cool against my bare feet. The tide is high but the water is calm. It slumps in soft pleats on the shore then is pulled away like a wrinkled sheet. I walk to where it laps at the sand and stand so that it skims the tips of my toes. Behind me is a glistening trail of footprints.

Plums grown by the ocean have a salty crust which offsets the devastating purple sweetness.

The water draws back like an invitation. I follow it over the wet sand and it hurries to meet me again, wrapping itself around my ankles and climbing up the backs of my legs. Not cold. Just cool. Like the underside of a pebble, or a word breathed onto a mirror.

The sea parts as I tread deeper and it closes behind me. I walk forward until I am submerged up to my waist. Over my head the ridiculous moon spins.

I reach up and untwist my hair from its tight, aching knot. I let it fall about my shoulders and it cascades like a cloak. It fans out and makes a halo around me on the ocean's surface, shot through with silver streaks of light. Its mass. Its heaviness. The salt-water weight of it. It drags my head back, as if the sea were sucking me under, eager to deliver me home.

My feet let go of the ground and I lean backwards into the waves and a hundred arms rush to catch me. Hands cradle my skull and slip beneath the curve of my back and the bends of my knees. Splinters of moonlight catch between my ribs and in the hollows made by my collarbones.

O my mother.

Carry me like a heart inside your chest and I will fold up my limbs under your breastbone.

I have drifted far from the shore. Above me is the deepest blue and below me a deeper one and I between, suspended by a thin membrane. I shed it, this itchy, ill-fitting human skin that I have borne so long, which catches on my scales and stretches taut over my gills like a winding-sheet pulled tight against nose and mouth. It falls from my body and underneath I am shining, effervescent. And I look down at my breasts my stomach my legs and all are silver. And I am beautiful.

And I am laughing.

I am powerful in the water. My body undulates with the waves and curves across the upturned face of the sea. And I can hear its song. And I tilt my head back and my ears are filled with the song and the song is joy and they have all come to sing it and they are all around me and their eyes are dazzling light. The water parts its lips around my head like a kiss.

O my ocean mother.

Open your arms and I will give you my name in one ecstatic breath.

"I wrote this after heartbreak caused me to spiral into the first big depressive episode I've suffered. I wrote it as a love story to myself and to anyone else going through heartbreak, to say that you should love yourself first."

JOSIE DEACON
Twitter @josiedeacon

Josie is a writer & digital gal from Scotland. She has a cat named Twiggy, and they live together with her partner in Edinburgh. Josie is animal mad and her fav animal is a squirrel!

His Eyes Were Green

HIS EYES WERE GREEN. Light and clear, a warm ocean to swim. I saw them on our third date. We were sharing a laugh and his eyes glistened. Slowly the colour revealed, like ink dropping into a bowl of water. I gasped at their beauty. He asked me what was wrong but I just smiled and said nothing. I took him home because I knew he was the one. I don't know when he saw my eyes, but he told me they were brown.

My favourite story from childhood is *The Princess Eyes*. I would cheer as The Princess and the Farmer saw one another and know it's love at first sight as they catch a glimpse of the colour of each other's eyes. My favourite part of films and books is when the protagonist realises they are in love and their interest's grey colourless iridises reveal their true colour. I dreamed of the day that would happen to me.

We dated for months, his eyes were getting clearer, the colour more vibrant. Flicks of golden brown appearing, the tint of blue in his green eyes gleaming. I was infatuated, I dropped everything. His were the only eyes I saw. But as his eyes became sharper, I felt myself fade. He grew distant, his temper quickening, his enthusiasm draining. I started to feel unloved, unwanted. He would say something and it would upset me, I'd cry for hours. Then he'd ring like nothing had happened. I was confused, I didn't understand what was wrong. His eyes were still green.

One day he texted me. "I can't do this anymore." And that was that. No goodbye, no explanation, only a severing of ties. It broke me. I had never felt like this: like all the life was being drained from my body. I was incomplete, fading from view and yet forced to live on, a colourless girl. I wanted it to stop. My whole body ached from crying. And then I felt hollow, like there was nothing left. Like I couldn't feel anything anymore. I was worthless, just an empty shell.

Time heals all wounds and eventually, slowly, I began to heal. The crying became weekly rather than daily, I ventured outside, walked the streets. But I was still looking for his eyes in the crowd. Looking for some colour, but there was none. My world had turned to grey.

I grew angry. How could he do this to me? Keep me around, falling deeper and deeper in love, forgiving everything he did, until he was the one to break us. I felt cheated, he was the bad one, I should have ended it. But I know I never would have, because his eyes were still the clearest green.

I went on dates but none of their eyes burst into colour by the third. I was holding these men to ridiculous standards, expecting everyone to give me the same rush that he did, for their eyes to reveal straight away.

I was fed up. I hated feeling like this. I got up and ran. I ran and ran until I was so out of breath I nearly fainted. I sat down, and let the rush of endorphins envelop me, warming me up, filling the hollow shell. I ran home and collapsed on the bed, smiling for the first time.

I continued running, I ate well, I started to do the things that I had loved before. I listened to music again, the songs didn't all remind me of him. I started again. A new life. My old life had revolved around his. My plans were based on where he was going to be. But now I was free to do what I wanted, to go where I wanted. I made a plan to go far far away, another beginning, volunteering on another continent. Become the woman I was meant to be.

The day of my flight I said goodbye to my flat. It was all packed up, ready for the tenants to move in. All that was left was the furniture for them to use, and my rucksack, filled with everything I'd need. I hoisted it on my back and looked at the mirror in the hall. I did a double take.

My eyes were blue.

"I wrote this version of Pandora's Box to see if she was brave enough to defy the expectations of the woman who despite everything could still have hope."

FREYA COTTRELL

Twitter @freyacottrell

Freya is an English Literature graduate who is currently travelling the world trying to find inspiration for stories whilst skilfully avoiding adult life.

Anesidora

THE MARKS PLASTERED HER SKIN. They marched along the
length of her arms and buried themselves in the crevices
of her elbows. They attacked her chest and made their way
towards her heart scarring her, branding her as the criminal
she was. They pulsed with every heartbeat and would sting
when she woke at night drenched in a cold sweat. The tops
of her legs had been spared, this perplexed her. The marks
that ran along her back irritated her most of all. She would
contort her spine and wrap her arms around herself so tight
that no breath could enter her, but she could never reach
the ones that itched the worst. She did not dare ask anyone
else to scratch them for her; then they would know what she
had done.

She had vague memories from a time before she had
them. Faces and colours. She remembered a craftsman
making clay figures. Men and women waiting for life to be
breathed into their naked clay forms. They seemed so very
important at the time. She remembered the wind. Hot and
humid. Blown from the lips of a goddess, it filled her being.
It began at her motionless feet and inched along her limbs

until she was full of it. She breathed it deep into herself and it made her heart race faster than it ever had before and faster than it ever has since. She remembered a beautiful woman, so beautiful that even the sun forgot to set in her presence. The woman's hands had cupped her pale cheeks, blown gently across her deep-set eyelids and run her fingers through her clay hair.

She turned her hair brown, made it thick and long. It draped over her shoulders and curled slightly at the nape of her neck. Then she was brought to a man who whispered in her ears. Gently he whispered sweet things: the yellow of the sun and the lilac of the flowers. And then he hissed cunning things: the green of the serpent and the red of the flame, she must remember these things. Then she was given a name.

Anesidora.

She would be forever known by this name. This infuriated and perplexed her. It was so basic, so futile, and so unnecessary. It was neither grand nor interesting. It was not insignificant or easily forgotten. It was mediocre. She was not mediocre. If she ever had the chance to name another, she would choose a name worthy of their future.

Her departure was lost in the void of memories. She was certain she had fallen endlessly until her face was no longer flushed from the heat of the beautiful woman's hand, until the cunning thoughts that the man had placed into her head were mere tendrils of wisdom that she had to cling to. She was presented as a gift to a man who was to become her husband. He reminded her of red, he would race through the world with no consideration to who or what stood before him.

He was a foolish man and she knew it. Someone had told her so. She was there to punish him for his foolishness and she knew it. Someone had told her so.

She could not remember whom it was that put the idea in her mind but it was so clear that she could think of little else.

Their union became sanctioned quickly and from it came a daughter. She named her Pyrrha. She was more radiant than yellow and prettier than lilac. Her daughter was destined for great things and she needed a name worthy of her future.

She had no possessions of her own, save the clothes on her back and a small box. The argent dress that covered her was the only piece she ever wore, it told of the beginning of the Silver Age.

The box was given to her by a man, an important man she could not remember. It shone slightly as she moved it in her hands; lilac to blue to green to pink. White lace protruded from the inside lining, hanging over its edge, small tongues licking her hands. It was cold to the touch. The box was the thing she treasured above all else. Above the memory of the beautiful woman, above the love she had for her daughter, and far above her foolish, foolish husband.

The box whispered to her. Its voice slipped into her thoughts and into her dreams until she had no other option than to wake, sit up, and listen to it calling and calling. *Anesidora. Anesidora.* How did it know her name? She felt cold flagstones under her feet, the blood rushed away from her head and small stars swam in front of her eyes. She would blunder into rooms and through archways until finally her vision cleared. In front of her was always the box. Her box. She mustn't open it.

The first time she tried, Pyrrha, her sweet Pyrrha, caught her hands and held them tight. She fought her mother for a long time twisting her wrists this way and that, covering her mouth so that her mother's screams wouldn't wake father. They mustn't wake father.

The second time her foolish husband knew she was coming. He waited for her. He held her box in his foolish, foolish hands. He dared to touch her only possession, the one thing in the world most precious to her. She felt his hands as though they were around her throat, rough and dirty. He clutched it tighter and her breath became shallow, so shallow, until there was no air left in her lungs at all. He let the box fall to the floor and she dropped to her knees, weeping.

The third time she watched as her pale fingers moved themselves of their own accord in front of her to the lid of the box. *Anesidora. Anesidora.* This time there was no Pyrrha to interrupt her, there was no foolish husband to stop her from doing what she had to do. The lid lifted. So easily. Too easily. And then they came.

A blur of darkness, a flurry of black, and everything she had ever dreamed was inside of her beautiful box was gone. They flew at her and bit her. Once: An ache of darkness washed over her body. Despair, misery, sadness. Twice: deeper and deeper each bite went until she felt them crawling inside of her, staining everything within her with their disease-ridden tongues. Three times: they tore at her clothes, biting and biting until her torso lay exposed, her silver dress turned to grey rags. They surged through the long, thick, brown hair the beautiful woman had blessed her with, pulling and tearing and turning it back to clay. They soared at her face, piercing her skin, stealing the blush from her cheeks.

And then, once they had had their fill, they sailed away. To travel to all corners of the world taking their disease and their sorrow with them. They left her on the floor ravished, broken and bleeding.

Her foolish husband came too late to help. He kissed her wounds, then beat her for her disobedience. She didn't care. The box had left its mark on her and inside of her. The black of despair. She rolled the new word around her mouth and tasted its bitter flavour. Despair. Poverty. Hunger. Disappointment. They were within her now and there was nothing her foolish husband could do about it. She clutched at her box while he continued to beat her. It called to her again. *Anesidora. Anesidora.* The voice was white, the white of the clouds. It was gentle and encouraging and Anesidora knew if she opened the box again Hope would be a part of her world once more.

She looked at her husband, her green eyes sparkling with malice. She let him beat her. She would punish her foolish husband. She was there to punish him for his foolishness and she knew it, someone had told her so.

She called her daughter to her and took a green ribbon from her hair, with it she bound the box. She would not let Hope escape.

This was her box to do with what she saw fit and she saw fit to keep it shut.

Soon the voice was no longer the white of the clouds, it had started to grey. It got weaker and weaker until there was little more of a gasp that called to her. And then it turned black. It screamed. It screamed and screamed. It screamed her name, it screamed its purpose, and it screamed all the vile things she had unleashed on the world. A long list. A reminder of what she had done. But she didn't care. She couldn't care. She just let it scream.

The sky turned black, the blood ran hot and thick and death hung in the air. Hope continued to scream. The box began to tire, its pearlescent sheen dimmed as the years of dust piled on top of it. The edges of the lace browned and curled inwards lapping up the dust on their dry tongues. The ribbon remained as green as the day she pulled it out of

Pyrrha's hair.

At first she visited the box daily but as the dust grew thicker she found the need to see it less and less. Hope never stopped screaming.

Anesidora didn't regret it. It was her box to open.

"I wrote this story for those facing adversity to show that you can succeed by understanding the rules of the game and using them creatively. This is about making your own opportunities, standing up to grotesque abuse and winning."

S.E. FENTON

Twitter @simonfenton1

S.E. Fenton lives in rural Berkshire, has his own small law firm and takes his spaniel, Dusty, to work. Honestly, she doesn't help much.

The Price of Fame

THE VEINS ON HIS CHEEKS were a vivid blue and he reeked of stale sweat and rancid cheese. His mean, pinched features, gnarled fingers and short, wiry frame were evidence that he was a survivor. He wore two jumpers, both with the elbows worn through, a tightly wrapped grey scarf and faded red woollen hat, with tufts of greasy white hair poking through. It may be that his looks caused people to be wary or that their wariness caused him to be brittle and reticent, but conversation was never comfortable for him or them. He was an unlikely shopkeeper.

He kept the shop just warm enough so ice did not form on the surfaces. There was a small wood burning stove in the middle of the room with as little coal as possible to keep it alight. At this time of year, the stove was failing to do its job. The front of the shop had pale green glass windows with a few items displayed, faded by the light. And because he could not sell them, he never changed the display. Around the other three sides of the room was an ebony counter with a hinged panel that lifted to allow him to pass through to the workshop and behind it were drawers in the same oppressively dark wood from floor to ceiling. A high rail bent evenly around the corners of the shop so a ladder could slide around the whole room. Every surface was polished smooth by years of wear. It was lit by a single oil lamp hanging from the ceiling near the shop door and giving off its own stench of burning whale oil.

A combination of the darkness, the cold and the shopkeeper's demeanour meant that visitors, finished with their business, left as soon as possible, not stopping to pass the time of day or gossip about neighbours. Still, customers knew that he was the most talented artisan of his generation.

It was just before six o'clock. He had been considering his supper for an hour or so when the bell above the shop door chimed loudly. As he came through from the workshop, he first noticed the steam coming off a skinny youth bending towards the stove. Was it a girl? Snow still perched on her hair. The grey and brown rags that posed as clothes were sodden. Her legs were bandaged where leggings should be and her feet slipped around in cracked and saturated clogs two sizes too big. He was about to shoo her out when she looked up and sideways and her smile staggered him. He was anticipating fear and apology. She was angelic, radiant. Her face reminded him of the painting of the Holy Virgin above the alter at St Gregory's. He smiled back. A rarity. He was instantly enchanted.

His food was ready in the back room and without a word

he brought her a steaming bowl of broth, a rough wooden spoon sticking out of it. It smelled of meat and onions and cabbage and the aroma filled the room. He held it in both hands and offered it to her with a small bow and she took it gracefully. She did not snatch. Without taking her eyes from his, she acknowledged his bow with a small nod of her own. He fetched a low three legged stool from behind the counter and placed it gently before her as he passed to lock the front door, turning the sign to say 'Closed'.

She sat, quietly eating the soup, savouring each small mouthful. He joined her in companionable silence, watching her. Nothing was said.

Eventually she handed him back the empty bowl and as he turned to place it on the counter he heard her say, 'Thank you sir.' These were the first words to pass between them and her voice was as perfect and light as her face. In a gentle voice he barely recognised as his own he asked:

'And how can I help you young lady?'

'I need your best dancing shoes.'

'Need, eh? And why do you need them?'

'Because with them I will become the finest dancer in the whole principality,' and as she said this she looked directly into his eyes. This could have been confrontational but it was not. He felt as if her equal.

He enjoyed her smile, her composure and confidence. He believed she could become a great dancer. Anyone can learn steps and moves and follow instructions, he thought, but she had something else too. She could be the object of love and admiration from those who had never met her, just as the statue of Aphrodite had excited men for generations. He could not take his eyes off her.

'And how will you pay me?' he enquired.

'You have a reputation for accepting "unorthodox" payment for your "special" shoes. And I know this is the only way I could obtain dancing shoes from the finest cobbler in the land'. The formality of her speech was inconsistent with her impression of dire poverty, but it only caused him to be intrigued further. This girl had a story; he knew it.

He smiled again, but the kindness and gentleness faded from his face as stark reality settled on him. The spell had been broken. He looked hard at her. His eyes narrowed as if he were stalking a deer with a crossbow and this was the moment just before he released the bolt into the unsuspecting doe's heart.

'You know the price?'

'Yes,' she answered in a firm voice. He had anticipated at least a small tremble.

'Tell me,' he demanded.

'After I have danced for a year and a day, you will come for my feet.'

'That is right.'

'I agree, but subject to one small request; when you have taken my feet, may I keep the shoes?'

He thought for a moment. No one had ever asked that

before. What could any of them have possibly done with dancing shoes and no feet to put them on? But the shoes would be frayed and dirty and he could not sell them anyway and so he agreed. He spat on the palm of his scarred and rough hand and she did the same and pushed hers, soft and pink, towards him. He shook it so forcefully her shoulder was yanked up and down. The awful bargain was struck.

After an uncomfortable moment he finally looked away, dropped her hand and peered up at the hundreds of small drawers on the walls. Eventually his eyes stopped on a drawer at the very top in the corner of the room.

'Red, I think,' he said, more to himself than the girl.

He marched to the ladder which had come to rest on the opposite side of the room and once in position beside it, he took a huge breath and shoved it with as much force as he had. The ladder flew around the room and came to a gentle stop perfectly placed under the drawer he had been staring at moments before.

He scuttled up with the swiftness and familiarity of a chimp in a circus and stretched to the drawer. He slid it open it and lifted out a brown cardboard box tied neatly with hairy string. He then amazed the girl by holding on to one of the railings, the box in his other hand, and hopped so that both feet touched the sides of the ladder at the same time. The result was that he slid to the floor in a second, blowing mites into the light of the oil lamp hanging by the door.

Such was the old man's disgust, he merely pushed the box at her. He could have fitted the shoes to her feet, but he could see her size and he knew his business.

And something about the transaction had angered him. Was it that the love and admiration and the warmth he had felt for the poor girl had been broken? All she wanted from him were his special shoes and she was prepared, just like all the others, to sacrifice her feet. He knew the contract was wrong and made him sick, but he was not in control. He had wanted something different from this one. There was a hope. It was only for a short moment, but it had been real and she had taken that away. He felt like a betrayed lover. He knew she had not led him on. She had not done anything really, but her eyes had promised so much. The anger and sadness and the pain in his stomach were real.

He knew he would not see her again until this time the following year. He stooped and unbolted the shop door, feeling defeated by the transaction. As he pulled it open, he was helped by the wind and sleet as it blasted in, rocking the oil lamp, causing dancing shadows to dash about the room. The girl walked out and into the night with a straight back, head erect. He watched her from the doorway as far as the corner where she turned down a side street and was gone. She did not look back. As he closed the door, he leant down to re-bolt it but had no energy to straighten up, so, with his back resting on the door, he slid slowly to the floor, his chest heaving as he quietly sobbed. Nobody heard.

* * *

He knew the pattern and was not surprised to have heard nothing about her for the next three seasons. As winter growled back into their lives, he started to hear stories of a beautiful dancer who captivated everyone who saw her perform. It was not only her feet which moved in a blur of precision and speed, but the look on her face, and how every single man and woman who saw her thought she was dancing just for them. Men were embarrassed by their red faces as they left the theatres. They knew their wives could tell who they would be thinking about in bed that night. Still, the wives too were consumed by thoughts of her.

* * *

Precisely one year and one day after her visit to the cobbler's shop, the girl was to dance for the Crown Prince at the Royal Opera House. There was no greater privilege. This is what she had always dreamed of. The audience was aflutter. Those who had seen her before spoke so enthusiastically to those who had not, that the anticipation pulsated throughout the building. Stagehands, violinists and ticket sellers alike were eager to catch a glimpse of the girl who was already a legend. As the fine gentlemen and ladies took their seats and raised their opera glasses, they did not know whether they were more excited to finally see the new star, or to get home to share the highlights with their neighbours who were not fortunate enough to get tickets. What a wonderfully sweet advantage.

The lights dimmed, the chatter became a murmur and eventually a silence as the conductor raised his baton. No one dared breathe for a long second. The overture began on the gentle movement of the conductor's arm with a single clarinet blowing a gypsy melody. Then another clarinet, and then violins. Musicians gradually joining the melody until finally the brass players blew and the hairs on everyone's necks stood tall.

The curtains were pulled open and a spotlight caught her standing completely still while the music swirled around the auditorium. For an impossible instant she was perched on the points of the toes of one foot like a statue.

And then it happened; she exploded into a leap across the stage like a firecracker busting into light. She spun and swooped and jumped and then stopped completely as the music paused, only her chest rising and falling from the effort. After three beats it started again, the orchestra and dancer in perfect unity.

The effect on those blessed to see her was the same as ever. Love, desire and admiration. She was dancing for him and for her. Alone.

It was like being caught in a breaking wave, they felt tumbled and upside down and disoriented, gasping for breath. And like being caught in a wave, it lasted forever and was over in a moment. The curtains closed for the twelfth and final time; twelve ovations. She had made so many people ecstatic by her dancing. In this past year, she had become familiar with the sensation and it was more profound than any other. She was beatific. And adored. And now rich. All in one year — because of those red shoes.

A towel was dropped round her shoulders by a blushing stage hand and she pranced off the side, running to her dressing room, filled with adrenaline and delight. As she pushed open the door with the silver star sparkling on it, she stopped.

He was sitting facing the mirror. He looked up and they stared at each other in the reflection. On his lap was a small axe, the handle made of the same ebony as his shop and the metal made of purest silver. At his feet was a box also made of the dark wood. The lid was open and it was lined with the thickest blood red velvet.

'How did you get in here?' She was not panicked. She was merely interested, because she had left strict instructions that tonight no one was to be allowed to bring her gifts.

'Does it matter?' he replied, coldly. 'You know why I am here?'

'I do. Let me help.'

This last comment caught him. 'Help?' No one had ever offered to help before. He had seen tears, been deafened by shrieks, and watched horror and terror on their faces. He'd had people begging to change the covenant. They did not believe he really would expect such payment. Not really. He had been attacked. He had been ambushed by the dancer's friends. They had fled, but never far enough. He had always been paid in full.

She sat on a purple padded chair next to him and rolled down her stockings. Past her muscled, milky thighs, to her strong and supple knees. Now it is he who shrieked. He launched himself backwards, toppling his chair, dropping the axe and stumbling over the wooden box. As the scream descended into a groan, the girl unstrapped the timber legs, articulated ankles and wooden feet from the stumps below her knees and offered them to the cobbler, her lips stretched into a serene smile.

'And I can keep the shoes, can't I?' she gently enquired.

"This story came about to shoe horn me out of winter solitude. It's about people coming together, which is how we can help each other out of darkness."

TALLULAH POMEROY

www.tallulahpomeroy.com

Tallulah is an artist and writer. She was born in London and moved to Bruton, Somerset when she was 11. She studied illustration at Falmouth. Later she illustrated for catapult.co and began making ceramics. She is fascinated by the human relationship with the natural world.

Coming out of Hibernation

I WASN'T READY FOR THIS.

Normally it's the winter that takes me unawares. Last year a draught blew in through the door-crack for months, the window rattled like teeth and snow kept blowing down the chimney. My clothes wouldn't dry. I shivered and shrivelled and waited for warm to return. Vowing that next year, next year I'd be prepared.

Now look; I'm layers deep in snug wool, thick from floor to ceiling. Smells of sheep and hay. I've hung glow-worm lanterns, and they sing to me. Back to my room and I muffle my way through wool, find the nook where I've worn it down into a hollow. Glow-worms in here too, tucked into gaps, making radiant spheres I can read by. These broken-spined books; these gentle worlds I've swum in for months. Deep stores of dried fruits and salted nuts, glace cherries. Yes, I really prepared myself for winter, I did winter well this year.

If it wasn't for the blaring of the birds outside.

I'm not ready for them. For the sprouting of the shoots

that force open my windows and writhe their greenly ways into my nest. I daren't look outside. Surely snow will fall again, and again, all will be quiet.

But spring seethes in, inexorably, up, open, out. I haven't the energy. I crawl to the casement and peep out. Oh, the yellowness of the sunshine smarts. Vibrant trees stretching into their new reddened tips, fairly bursting to spew out buds. Glorious trumpet-flowers in their yellows, tootling their trumpet-sounds for all to hear.

Don't get me wrong, I don't hate spring. I love the rising of the sap, the joy of new life, it's just that I'm not sure I'm ready yet. The glow-worms have hatched into crackle-winged dragonflies and they're zipping about my room, butting into the wool, getting their fine selves tangled in the threads.

I open the window wider to release them. A breeze catches me. Sure, it stirs something. Memories. Something in my bones that seems from long, long ago, an ancient waking. As if I could become someone quite else, if I were only to leave my nest.

I cloak myself in wool and inch out the door. Smells assault me from all sides; acrid pollen, insect juice, fresh wet moss. I am a secret bush of wool, in camouflage, I hope nobody knows who I am. I don't feel like small talk. How was your hibernation? they'll say. Woolly, I'll say, and yours? Oh, also woolly, and we'll continue on our way. Rather not bother.

It's the urgency of it that's getting to me. Why the rush? Why the buds bursting from the branches with such force? The rising of the sap like a volcanic explosion through the fibres of the trees. The interweaving leaves, puffing out into fullness, stretching themselves suddenly into full existence when just the other day it was all so still and quiet. I liked it that way. The solemnity of the bare trees against the darkened sky. My ruminations. I haven't even nearly finished my ruminations, let alone the Tudors, and here I am being brushed on all sides by new ideas growing out of the ground faster than you can blink. I shuffle at a very slow pace to show the spring I'm my own person. I don't follow the crowd. Sheepish, I am. I decide that will be my verb for the spring. I shall have a sheepish spring.

Ada took me by surprise. She was hiding in the hedgerow. I'd poked my head out of the wool to dry my face, for my breath had condensed somewhat, and she spotted me. Her face was terribly bright. Her arms full up with round pennywort. Yellow gorse flowers tucked in her hair.

"Oh, hello," she said, "would you come with me and have some hedgerow soup?" My stomach moved around a bit, saying, yes, we have had enough of dried things. "Pick some sorrel," she said.

So I gathered those slender leaves, and touching them was a little electric at first, my fingerprints buzzing like circuitboards. My wool was getting caught on the gorse. Dew soaking me up to the knees. I'll go back to my nest after soup.

Ada's house is underneath a mossy bank, a long low old place with a door that hangs off its hinges somewhat. Roots trail in from the ceiling. There are gaps for the sky to peep in. I can't think how she got through winter. But it's got a certain rustic charm. She's made all the stools herself. It's wise to check them before you sit, for some are wobbly.

On the wany-edged shelves line rows of jars, with green things floating in them, yellow, brown. Ada chooses one and pours it into a cup for me. The soup begins to bubble on the stove, the greenly smell of it, dampening my shrivelled skin. I sip at my cup; it tastes like soil.

In through the door comes the bony figure of Edwin in his yellow coat. He raises his eyebrows at me silently which means, well, aren't we all here then, what a to-do! He takes out his mandolin and begins to play while the soup gets greener. I close my eyes. There are sounds that touch your nerve-endings and make them warm. I let the warmth suffuse my spine. Shake the wool down from my head that I may feel more with my ears.

I hear the door creak again and I don't open my eyes, but I know it's Ulrika because she's laughing, that full rich laugh, croaky from lack of use but you can still tell it's her. I find myself trying to smile. An unfamiliar sensation. My cheek-muscles have almost atrophied and I can see I'm going to have to get back into shape if this social interaction is going to continue.

Ulrika has climbed onto the table beside the stove and is dropping wood-ears into the soup. "They're very good for you," she says when Ada looks hesitant.

"Are you sure they're not confused with something poisonous?"

"Yes I'm sure, there's nothing even faintly like them"; and it's true, I have never seen mushrooms that look more like ears. Velvety ears. She throws me one and I put it to my own ear. It sounds like a mouse's whisper. The mandolin goes quiet.

"Is it annoying?" Edwin asks. "Should I stop?"

Ulrika laughs with her head tilted back and says, "There will be no stopping anything today!"

My cheek-muscles twinge. Edwin resumes his song. I wonder if the soup will be ready soon, but Ada says we're waiting on Jan with the bread. And we know what Jan's like. He'll have grown his beard down to his waist now, and be talking to all the birds and the lambs and the girls he meets on his way.

When the door swings open again, that flash of bright sunlight on the floorboards, glinting off the jars, I think it's him but it's not; it's the short figure of Mary Weddon with her round glasses and the gap in her teeth and her way of shaking your hand which makes you feel so secure. She pats me on the head and the shoulders and I feel a bit of winter shake out of me and roll under the cupboards. In the deep pockets of her corduroy trousers she has bottles of something brown she's brewed all winter. Pops the caps for us with her teeth and they tingle under our noses.

"Well," she says, "robust. How was your hibernation?"

Ada says she learned the stars and got chilblains. Edwin says he grew immensely lonely and made up songs about imaginary friends. We ask him for one. He sings in a thin mournful voice; "O Eliza, Eliza, my yellow-haired Eliza, how I love to sing with you Eliza." It's not the most inspired of lyrics, but doesn't sound like he had much to work with.

Ulrika turns circles among the pots and pans and says this is the most movement she's done in months and it feels wonderful. Her bones creak in their sockets. I want to tell them about the glow-worm lanterns which turned into dragonflies but they seem like part of another world so I just say, "Woolly. It was woolly."

A moment of quiet arrives like a calm patch of lake, spreading into reflection. We lean against each other, some standing, some sitting, some heads in laps. I absently pull gorse from Ada's hair. It feels nice to have bodies beside me. Edwin plays one long note on his mandolin. We all think about Eliza.

The soup has greened its most greenish green and still no bread.

"Jan," says Ada, "typical Jan, he'll be rolling around in the clearing with some beauty, palms full of clover and celandine, forgetting all about the hedgerow soup. We'll start without him."

Ada ladles it into bowls and it smells so good.

"That smell could wake the dead," says Edwin, "we'll have hosts of them at the door."

And Ada says, "Well, they're welcome, the dead don't eat a lot."

At this the door seems to rattle, and we move aside a little to make way for anyone who might want to shelter here with us. Ada has a very open-door policy. She tips fermented garlic buds from a jar and gives us three each. They are potent.

Our bowls are empty and the light has sifted down into dusty amber. There's that scent coming in from outside, one I've not smelled in so long, although it must come every year it takes me back to some time long ago, maybe even before I was born – the smell of what has been sunshine on green things, on soil, then becomes dew, and the mingling of the two is that tangy acid dampness. We all seem to smell it at once, Edwin stands and stretches his long limbs over his head, crinkling up his yellow coat, Ulrika lets out a long happy sigh, Mary collects the bowls and drops them into the sink (now is not the time for washing up, not today) and we go outside.

It's a powdery sort of evening. The urgency of this morning has calmed, thank goodness, we did enough today, the sap may stay where it is for a minute while we take a breath. Sure, the trees are taking a breath, the grass is taking a breath, and letting it out in a long dusty exhalation.

There's a thin moon-rind already visible, and behind the crisscross of bare twigs stars are starting.

We are quiet, there's nothing needs to say. We are here, winter finished, as always it feels at once returned and new, this ringing similarity and strangeness. Now it's unthinkable I spent so long enwooled. Alone, inside! No, I shall not do that again, not for a very long time. A dragonfly whirrs onto the brim of Edwin's hat. And out, into the misting sky.

By the time Jan finds us it's almost dark. He's singing to himself, something wide and wordless and fairly tuneless too. Laughs at us all, sat against the bank in quiet. I had business to attend to, he says, with a hint of a story to be told, and we see flowers plaited into his long white beard, pollen on the deep valley crinkles of his eyes. Brings a loaf out of his jacket pocket, still warm, we pull it apart and take care to drop some on the floor in case the dead are hungry after all.

"I love mermaids. But in traditional stories, mermaids tend to reflect the male gaze. Beautiful, elusive, vain, dangerously seductive – they identify female sexuality with the lure of the sea itself. I wanted to write a story from the mermaid's point of view that reflected how women often experience their own bodies, as painful, awkward, confusing. I wanted my mermaid to be a woman who loves women, a heroine whose story is about finding love in her own shape."

SARA FAIRLIE
Twitter @LearNonsense

I teach at the University of St Andrews, writing literary non-fiction by day (my book Inventing Edward Lear was published by Harvard University Press in 2018) and fairytales with a comic, political edge by night. Working on a novel, The Princess Unlucky in Love.

Dollfin

TIME WAS. SEA, SKY, SEA. I flowed. I floated. My sleek skin shining. It was beautiful. I was beautiful. The way things are that only are. No knowing why. I leapt and the sun struck me silver. I dived and stars bloomed round me.

We moved in a chord. Waves. Up, up, up-through-the-air, and down, down, down-through-the-water. When we laughed you could hear it for miles. Booms and chuckles and clicks. A ricochet of jokes.

Food swam into my mouth and I swallowed. At storm season we lived low. Murky sometimes. Weed, sand, sudden strange stalk-eyes rushing through tunnels. Mouthfuls of grit. Bully waves. Rib-punching, sweeping you up and knocking you down. Catching the rip and shooting for the sandspit. Too near sometimes. Breathless. Almost into the outer space where you grow heavy and there is no air. Where goggle-frogs with nets.

One of us broke a piece of coral and we chased it, caught it, saw it spin and sway as it feather-fell, side to side, waving at the water's will to the seabed. I liked to watch things fall that way, gently.

One was a boat-nose, nosy. He led us on wildflights. Chasing boats, plucking deadfish out of the dead air. Up on our tails. Throwing shapes through the sunlight. Dodging away before the odd-frogs topple, like sticky coconuts flailing into our sweet water, trying to touch us.

So, I love-lived, all one race, racing, tail-flicking, bow-arch smile – end to end. A muscle rainbow. A sine. We knew where we were with each other. Always. Touching. We wove ourselves through the sea-waves, boat-wakes, light-flakes.

Then someday, a heaviness. Behind my eyes. A gut-ache, as if I'd swallowed a marlin, spike inward. A crab-thing scuttling in my innards, a drag in my spine. A little blood (from where?) ghosting in the water. Dancing into nothing. I thought I was dying.

Others nose-nudged, laugh-talked, flipped me the tail. Kind, mostly, wanting to buoy me. Swam me to the surface to see the sea-gleam when the light rose, shell-colour, and everything was made new. They waited. The hardest thing, the swim-but-not-move. Letting two tides a day wash in and out. Weighted.

But I was not of their kind. Not any more. I couldn't explain. My laugh was shrinking. My nose was going wrong. And, worst, a tumour-bulge, two gross lumps of flesh, were growing over my heart, so it could touch no-one directly ever again. I was not clean. No free flight more through the bright blue curve of day. I was barnacled, streaming with weed. I told them to go. Go. I hated the pity in their ever-laughing eyes. It was disgusting. I was disgusting. A crusted anchor, with two prongs suddenly, that flailed and flapped. And odd-colour. Odd-frog sun-sore. The pall of dead-fish-flesh, but on the outside. No shine. Only my fluke was still glossy and grey and fast.

I starved, almost. I couldn't nose fish. Until I was as thin as an eel and lashing out at anything, and suddenly I found I could seize fish with my flippers, dart out at them and lunge and bring things to my teeth and that way feed. The firm fresh flesh of a mackerel was a joy in my mouth. Sweet, oily. But I couldn't swallow it whole, as before. I must grind it in my mouth. Learning how took months. Lonely.

I made my way to the rocks where we dived once for squid. I love squid. Love the sucking-in noise when you gulp them down, the soft streamers tickling your mouth. And I thought, my head has become a squid: it is covered in streamers that float. And the notion came to me somehow to drag it off. So, I found a rock, and I swam upright, fluke down, and I used my flippers to drag a rock through the tendrils on my head, trying to scrape them away.

That's when they saw me. A boat with odd-frogs. Jeering and whooping. 'It's a Mermaid! Giveus a fishlove! Titsa Hoyden! Get her, lads!'

I slipped back down. But my back was grazed in my slitherfright and I was wild with panic. Thrashing about. Three times they tried to net me. The boat driving me back onto the rock. Then they came too close and a grinding noise, the boat keeled and they were in the water with me. I had not known fear before then.

The lunge of them toward me, the drag of their fin-gear, eel-mouths, clawing to stay up, trying to pull me back to them as if I were a fish they wanted to eat and at the same time cling to. Things fall into the water and drop. Creatures dive into the water and flow. But the odd-frogs neither dropped nor flowed. They fought. They were not up or down. They writhed and spat and shouted and cried. The tide tossed two of them onto the rocks, where they lay and bled and shivered. The others became still and almost-dead, and then quite-dead, black. The eyes crusted with salt, staring.

I was sick and shiver-shot, though the sun was hot and the sea was all sun-quiver and gentle rocking. Orcas I knew to flee. But odd-frogs who gave fish and laughed and were so brightly coloured I had thought like birds who skimmed the water-top for a time and then flew off, who knew where, wave-bouncing, screeching to colonies of noise. We chased their wakes lightly. I had not nosed danger.

Now the cold current of a deep-sea trench flowed through me. I swam hard and long, as far as far – and retched always the taste of rot in my mouth – til I reached some better bay. A place I liked for the sand-shine below the surface and the way the land scooped and swooped from peaceful shallows to a huge coral forest.

This is the first place I know I was with my mother, my kin, before I grew. Blue and yellow stripe flights of fish like bubbles out of my mouth. Waving fronds. Tunnels of pink and green, always dancing with crab and shrimp. My first octopus. Sand-rock still, then whoosh-balloon away, orange-red, swirling ink. My mother laughing at me as I hugged her flank.

The water smelled sweet here. The sun was kind on my back. I healed. I hated my new form, so unglide. Uglied. The blood that came with the moon-tides and brought sharks nosing into the cove, so I had to drag myself half-out, onto rocks in a sea-cave, till the tide turned and the round ache in my belly withered to a glinting sliver. But I found new pleasures.

My fin-gear, so clumsy for diving, could pick up shells and let them fall, side to side. I gathered periwinkles, scallops and seaweed, weaving them around my head, my body. I swam simple stitches in the warm-clear waves. I heard whale-song, far out in the night, and sometimes – with a sad-lovely scatter of memory fresh as snow on sea-ice – I made out the twanging chatter, the slides and crackles, and laughing echoes of my own people. No certain words. Just the sing-tones of travel banter.

Quietly, I began to sing myself. The noise was strange in my blunt-toothed mouth. It did not move through water at all, as if my tongue had become thick. But when I thrust my head out of the water, in the night air, I found a relief in calling. I do not know who I was calling to. I could not understand my own voice. I made the sounds of the wind, of birds, of the sea-sigh on the sand. Hushshsh. Nobody ever came there, to that bay so steep-shouldered.

Until one waning of a flat, hot day I was enjoying the cooler lift of the air as the sun sank octopus-red and I heard laughter, light and high, a squeal, almost that of my own kind. A splash. Fast-thrash arms of one chasing another through water for fun. Breathless laughter.

I couldn't make much out. They were odd-frogs and I was scared. Still, I went closer. Maybe they were children. Something about them gave play. And I did not think they could see me.

I swam low, deep, stealthy, without breathing as if I was rounding up fish. There were three of them. Odd-frogs certainly, with four-prong fin-gear and bodies with picture-patterns like boats. But bowsprit-slender, light-voiced, gentle. Fear-males.

As I came closer my good sea-sense began to drain from me and I felt light, humorous almost. I wanted to surprise them by doing a leap, or shooting between them, brushing their bodies for a second before bow-arching and lighting out to sea as fast and confusing as a cloud of ink.

I wavered, swimming on my tail with my head up, but close against the rocks. I listened. They spoke. Joked. Silvery somehow. Moon-toned. Their eyes gleaming with spree.

They swam in a ring, their fin-gear waving gently like an anemone feeding. They tried to touch the bottom and burst up to the surface gasping, as if it were hard for them to get so far down. They sang. I was amazed by how free they seemed and happy. It was the first time I had thought that creatures who lived both on land and sea could be truly in either place.

When they finally left, I did not sleep. It was the same as on those nights, far out at sea, when the waves glowed and we jumped through them, seeing our own bodies flash green till dawn.

They did not come the next night. Rain blew in suddenly and the bay was grey as my tail. The day hung heavy with me. The fish ran, but I felt no desire to grasp them. My short-smile face was salt-tempered, parched. The light stung my eyes. I watched the steep shoulders of the bay. Birds wheeled, scolded, settled. Small furred creatures twitched heads out of holes, then fear-fled back into the land's belly. I swam down, surfaced, scanned shore: over and over. They did not come.

Three more days. Nothing.

Then a sand-shine day, the sun like a turtle egg hot-hatched from the moment of its beginning. I saw boats like stretched clouds skimming the sea brim. I heard them return over the rocks before I saw them: their musical voices chattering and laughing as they carried something down to the shore.

They made a pile of rocks and driftwood. Then they lit it up, as if the sun was caught in it, though it was almost dark. These graceful odd-frogs ate and drank by their crackling tangle of sun. Then they stripped their skins and slipped into the water. Something had made them bold. They swam much further than before, out of the shallows, into the cool deeps where subtle currents slink and drag.

I followed, enchanted. I wanted to touch them, to be one with them. It made me think of early days, when we swam with one mind, bending to fill each other's spaces, completing each other's lines. Chasing wakes, bouncing off the race of bubbles, up, up, up and swooping down, down, down.

So, I followed, staying under. Listening. Watching their pale odd-frog fins waving in the water. How badly they swim, these split-tails! Yet they are sweet in their hopelessness, crawling and bobbing and fighting the tide. I wanted them, wanted to touch one of them. They were so beautiful and free. Grey twilight; the cool, sweet out-breath of a stifling day.

I surfaced a little away, watching them lie on their backs and stare at the stars. Something different about their talk today – looser, wilder, nothing-laughs and sudden silences. They seemed as if they were spinning. Though they were not moving very much, the dusk whirled, like when you come too near a boat's spinner. Whatever mood they were in, I caught it. Reckless. I swam closer, close.

Then one of them saw me.

'There are four of us,' she said, 'Look.'

'We're so stoned we're seeing ghosts.'

'What the hell! Where did she come from? There's nothing here.'

'That's so weird...'

'Say something'

'Hello! Hell-oh-oh!'

'Is she real? Is she deaf?'

'Hey girl! You on holiday too?'

They stared. Nobody blinked. I could not breathe. They thought that I was one of them. A terrible understanding took me. I wanted to shout 'NO!!!!' and yet something deep down also answered yes. I could not help nudging one with my tail. She screamed. Then they panicked. Thrashing back to land. One caught herself on a rock, painfully. She screamed.

'I'm bleeding. I can't swim!'

One of the others had already staggered out. The second turned, dazed, in the water, flailing. She could not see well enough. Or was too confused.

'A-lease-ya?' she shouted.

She, too, got on land amongst the rock-shapes and the wood-glow.

'Help me! Oh god...it hurts. I can't SWIM.'

I was turning circles through the churned water around her, wildly, angry in myself for wanting to touch, swimming too close. I did not want this odd-frog to lie on a rock and turn black from the sight of me, till her mouth was all sand-flies and her eyes burst. Surely I was not so terrible – so ghastly. Why did I damage? What mute-hate had seized me and monstered me so I could not touch without making terror? So ugly even by moonlight.

At first the odd-frog was struggle-heavy, heaving, water-clawing, rasp-gasping like an orca stormswept onto sand. Then quieter, moaning, drifting out into the cold-current. I was fear-full. But I swam below her, fin-gear under hers, holding her head high. She was so heavy it drained me, yet I also loved the cold-warm drag of her soft skin. Touching as little as might be to not-know-me from the waves below. Vague as mist, quiet as stars, I swam almost without breathing, trying to bring her to shore without beaching my own body. Nosing. Nudging her through the shallows. And with one final push, up onto a slab of stone where I saw her roll over and retch, the water pouring from her mouth like dry sand out of a shell.

In the morning, they were gone. Afterfordaysallwasdarkwithinme.

I swam in the green, cold deeps where there are beings without names, even without bodies. Graveyards of bleached coral that turns to dust when you touch it. Algae cobwebs. Grey rot, clear shapes that hang and drift like jellyfish, but are not alive. And I was not in my body. I was scum. Sick, dull-fleshed, floating. I was not for myself. I was not for anyone. I had no kind. I was a trap. Not just a fish-eater but a false fin, dangering boats. A part-frog, doll-fin mermaddle. Disgusting in desire. Vain.

I drifted. The rains came, strafing the waves grey. Clearer air. Sooner dark. Soothing. Boats were less and the water-top safer. I rose when I wished and looked about long times. Birds with red beaks, posted in rock-holes on a stool-splashed sea-stack, diving for eels. Pink stone, grey stone. A strand of round pebbles. I came to a place I had not swum before. Where dappled fatsels lay grunting on the rocks, in families, land-blubbering – salt-snort and high-crying moan of company. I fished with them sometimes. They did not mind me.

This place was sea-circled, safer. Just one boat-cove. No odd-frogs dwelled there. I was sure. Maybe once, but not now. I liked the silver light, which falls only where there is empty. The sky like a dark mussel opening a crack to show its water-pearl. The soft sheen of peace.

I was wrong, though, about odd-frogs. After the snow-fall, in the green season, there was a boat. I saw it putter in and tie tail. I hid amongst rocks, far out, but close enough to see. Six stepped out, all with coloured humps, which they dropped on the beach. Fear-male. They threw and caught a skim-thing, running here and there, calling out in fresh voices, high with delight. Then they made the coloured humps into peaked red and blue caves that flapped and sang as the wind whipped them. Then two of them ran white-limbed into the water, split-chest pricking hard with pleasure, screaming 'It's so COLD!!!!' and whooping as if they'd caught a shoal of herring.

My fluke froze. Fear crawled up from my gut. I knew that I would harm them or they me. Stay away. Stay. Away. I told this to my mix-taken body. I made myself swim far out, tiring my heart with fierce strokes. I caught more fish than for a week before, so hungry-fixed I was on hunting, so high on the current that flowed in me of not-looking at those beautiful split-tail, split-chest odd-frogs – so like me above, so unlike below. I could not danger them. I swam away. I swam back. I played false by my own resolve. I bargained with myself. The end of that wrestle was I came only at night.

I heard them before I could see anything. A strange music came from the red cave, lit within. Something tugged and something held. Tugged and held. As the eye moves from one star to the next, so this music moved across the air, each sound skipping to one near it. I was in its charms at once. Netted. There was no voice that I could recognise. Just sounds, sweet as water. I needed to know what made that noise.

I swam as close as I dared, leaned my back up against the hard stone of the cove and let my tail beat the water softly. There was laughter. A fin-clap ripple. Then low-voice chat. At last they ventured out of the cave, all bearing sticks, at the ends round moons of white light that danced on the rocks and shore. The one who made music strummed and hummed; she had a curving paddle-box, a body of wood with a long neck that she plucked and stroked and held, as if it were a baby, but one that spoke her thoughts.

'It's so magical here!'

'Thousands of stars. They must be there in the city, but you never see them.'

'Yeah. Pity it's not warmer. I'd skinny dip.'

'Dare you!'

'People. It's not safe. It's the wine talking.'

'What does wine say?'

'Let me breathe!'

'Precisely.'

'What do you mean?'

'I mean I'm going in.'

That was the music bringer, with a low-laughing voice.

'Don't be daft! Wait until the light at least...'

'I'm not sure about this.'

'You're never sure.'

Now they were all six in the water. Pleased and shocked at their own doings.

'Hold hands. Nobody go far.'

'Ouch! Sharp pebbles.'

'Whose idea was this?'

'It's freezing!!!!'

They laughed. 'Let's gggget ooout!'

Five of them splashed back the few yards up the sea-tangle, wrack and shell, their soft white flesh like squid. So unfitted to the hard shore, stone-heap, cut-bruise of land. Scuttling into their red caves. Only the music bringer stayed out a few beats longer. She swam a few strokes toward where I was, as if scenting something.

I became the rock. I did not breathe. She was near now. Two boats' length. I closed my eyes, so that they could not catch the moonlight. In a moment I would dive. Then she threw a pebble. Not hard, but skimmingly. Plop, plop-plop, plop. Right at me.

I was so surprised that I tail-splashed, fluked right at her. Then I swam for my life. I stayed away for a whole day. Far out to sea. Scared shiftless. I was well warned. Yet I could not help returning. Maybe they would catch me. Maybe I would die. It was all one. I wanted to see her again.

That day was rain. Clam sky, shut. Wind rippling the red caves and the blue, their light bodies. A day for hiding. I saw two of the odd-frogs in bright yellow skins, digging. Not her. Where was she?

I arced and dived and caught fish without thinking. Then I saw it. Out where my rock was, in the curve of the cove. Something high up. Left for me. I swam fast underwater, surfaced noisily. I had to hoist myself on fingear-point to reach it, making myself seeable almost to the tip of my tail. I didn't care.

I pulled it down. It was a circle of sea-pinks. The little flowers that grow in rock, in odd places, high up. Beautiful. Woven so clever you could see no end. I put it on my head. But then I could not dive or I would lose it. So I put it back. Tried it on again. Looked about to see if there was someone there. But there was nobody.

That night I hid in a sea-cave and broke coral into small and smaller pieces, robbed mussels of their tiny inner moons, rubbing my fin-gear sore until I had a sea-strand of weed and shell and stone that shone. I left it in a rockpool, so it would stay shining. Near the point where she had seen me. Would she find it?

Waiting was like breathing with bruised ribs. Pain. Pleasure. Pain. No choice. Then she was there, out in the sun-bright early, with a fellow-frog, blue-backed and black-toed. Clambering. I could hear them chatter, words carry on the salt air.

'Sometimes I think I see a dolphin the bay.'

She smiled. 'I doubt it. Maybe one of the seals.'

'Maybe.'

She wasn't looking my way. But she knew I was there. I just knew.

I dived, thrashing the water with my tail as I left, so she would know I was leaving in anger. When I ventured back, the sea-strand was gone. In its place a secret, not of the sea or of the land. Like a clam, a thing that was shut and opened. Inside a silver moon so bright-shine it dazzled.

I dropped it; dived for it again. Screwed up to look at it. Inside was a creature, big-eyed, wondering back at me, like an eel from a rock-hole. Scared, I shut. After, opened. Over and over. Only when a salt-sting came in my eye and I brushed it I saw the same in the moon. Drew my fin-gear over my mouth, my nose, through my salt-bleach fronds. Down the gully of my neck. My eyes are wrack-green. My out-stuck ears shell-whorls. I am...something. I do not know what. Ugly or lovely. Both. But this thing gave me back myself.

I heard them talking.

'I could live here,' she said.

'For a week. But tell me you're not missing a shower.'

'I'm not missing a shower.'

'You're weird. There's nothing here. It's glorious – don't get me wrong. But my phone is out of juice. I've got sand in my socks. I can't wait to put on some lipstick and heels and go to a bar and...flirt a little. Creature comforts.'

'I know what you mean,' she said. But her eyes were sparkling and her cheeks were red. 'One more day. It's supposed to be fine, too.'

Something about the way they were looking out to sea told me. They were going. Packing their red and blue crab-caves on their backs and riding the boat away. Where families. More-boat coves. Rock-colonies as high as clouds. Where odd-frogs shoaled like herring.

A pang went through me. Lose her. My belly was full of stones. Why could I never care for the things that stayed? For rock, sand, rain. I had met but had not touched her. I wanted to see the colour of her eyes.

I could not leave the bay. I hungered, did not feed. I could not bear to miss the moment of their going.

And it came. They shouldered their shells, clattering with gear, busy with move-meant, un-travelling the days here, rebonding to new-old places. Each made her own wave. A sign, a look, a little mound of pebbles left at the tidemark. Then they walked over the dune grass and lost to view. But she not yet.

'I'll see you at the boat,' she said. First, she sat on the stones with her split-tail folded like a gull's wings. She strummed on the paddle-box, plucked and stroked and held it. I swam as close to the beach as I could without stranding. She saw me, smiled, played on. 'Til I felt she was weaving music to me, catching at me with her fin-gear. Star notes fell in the clear water, with the gullscream around us, and the shallows blue-green in bright sunlight, as fish are in the striped deep.

She put down the box. Then stripped skin, fast and handy. And she came in to me. With a skitter on the hard stones, and a half-dive. She swam well when none watched: fast, easy strokes. Hardly pushing the water. Face under. Long streamers of dark, wet pooling round her white skin as she rose near me.

'Hello there,' she said, and looked long.

Then she reached for me. I splashed away. Nobody touches me like that. Fin-gear to fin-gear. Yet I wanted her to come close again. She swam to me, softly. Keeping her fin-gear on the water-top, where I could see them. In and out, in and out. We stayed. Just swimming and looking, two seals' breadth away.

Her eyes were browngold fleck, like a seal's. I was glad to know that, to hold it like the secret moon-clam she gave me that told my own. I made the motion of opening it, to show her, and smiled. She smiled back.

Then she swam right up to me, until our heads were tangled and her frank, hot mouth was on mine, and it was a pleasure-dream of floating free, that I had not felt since I lost my long-laughing sharp-nosed, rainbow self. Still even as we twined our fin-gear I kept my tail behind me, out of the way. I minded it. It, fluke-flopped and flapped from side to side. Rough, shiny. Cool skin where our heads were hot. Too fishy to bring near her, too shy-bold in its needs. Different from her soft white split-fins. Did I smell of oil, of mackerel? I cannot now say when it happened. But having closed-eyes to kiss and kiss again and drawn my fin-gear down her perfect nose, and lips and chin, I looked down suddenly into the water and saw what I knew but didn't believe. Her fluke, twining, curving, gently beating the water. She was as I was. Laughing.

'There are more of us than you'd think.' No different. Split-chest bobbing on the water-top, strong tail cutting through the current. Nothing to choose between us. I dived beneath to see her whole, and it was as if I was visiting my own mix-taken form and re-viewing it, beautifurling through the sun-shadow of weed and rock, creatures and boat-bits fallen or thrown into the wonderful wash of the world. Perfect.

I wanted to ask how she went on land, how she passed. But the sun was falling already, and I knew that she would go. Taking her music with her. That the boat would come and tie tail and when it puttered, turning, out of the cove I would forever be looking for the sign of a wake.

'I said I could live here', she held me and whispered, 'and I meant it. I'll be here again. But...' I swam a little from her. Salt-eyed, a bubble of happiness about to burst, turning to gravel. Aglow and aghast. 'You have to find your own way out.'

And with that she turned and dived, fluking farewell, and swam hard at the beach till I saw her stagger. As if carrying sand in each limb of her odd-frog, split-tail self. She balanced. Righted herself. And strode up the shingle, loudly, not looking back.

"The story is about lies. About how they can often be a more comfortable place to live and love. I wrote it because the most powerful falsehoods we tell are to ourselves. Even when the blanket of them is removed, often the moment we get the chance, we will fall under it once again."

KRISTELLE BENUWA
Twitter @kristelbuckleyx

Kristelle is a writer and an actress who splits her time between London and the North East. Her work centres around lies and relationships, but primarily identity - a result she credits to her mixed raced heritage. She's also a sucker for a good love story.

I'll Find You

"WHAT ARE YOU THINKING?" He spins a chocolate coil of her hair between his fingers.

She stares into space. Her face is one that if she does not focus on its arrangement, it will go wherever her mind does, contorting into the emotion needed for her internal adventure. In this second, it is focused; her groomed brows wrinkle ever so slightly, and the corner of her lips turn down. Her expression stills and her eyes flicker as she skips between thoughts.

His words anchor them in his direction, golden irises propelling her body toward him. The tension falls from her face and a smile spreads on her lips.

"Nothing of consequence," she leans forward before he has the chance to respond, giving him a chaste kiss that functions as a full stop.

She returns to her former position, closing her eyes.

He sighs, raising and dropping her head with the rhythm of his breathe. She shifts, placing a quick peck on his bare torso. *Don't worry, my love. There is nothing on my mind.*

He moves now, sitting up in such a way as to not disturb

her, but enough to drop another kiss into her hair, savouring the scent of strawberry and riches that clings to her mess of curls. *I know that's not true, but we'll talk in the morning.*

The message is clear and she nestles into him, stealing the warmth that emanates from his body. With the arm that arches around her, he pulls the bedspread over her shoulder, and prepares himself for sleep.

Aria and Jack have been a pair for some time. They are in love. That much is certain, and at its simplest, that is all there is.

Jack is the captain of his ship. To give him another fitting title would be wrong, though many had been assigned to him. He travels to travel, he sails for the love of sailing, and for the hatred of home. He is a young man, a young handsome man, with an inherited fortune and an air of confidence that when worn the way he does is defined as arrogance. But he is kind, and he wears his self-importance, he does not internalise it. He is a man of charming words and few secrets.

The woman he holds is entirely different. Deception is ingrained in her, so much so that she cannot recognise honesty. Even her name is not her true one. Aria, in her essence is forged by secrets. She is proud and she is beautiful. Silken brown tresses, gilded eyes and skin of the shade of soft oak. Nobody says no to Aria.

Yet they love one another. Very much. For him, she is home, and for her, he is the one thing that she can trust.

Which poses the issue. Maybe if the world were different, they could have continued this way. But there is one thing that Jack did not know about Aria, a secret that made her desperate to look for any reason to relinquish her faith in him.

He had given her no reason to do so, not yet. So, she thinks instead on their destination, an island that hid just beyond the horizon. Silently, she repeats the instructions given to her until her façade becomes her truth, and they are both asleep.

* * *

It is not hard to find. The cave that the cabin girl had spoken of was not a humble place. A bearded man, large and imposing, perches upon the cliff face. Though carved from the rock, he looks as if he may fall, a foot precariously hovering halfway down the wall, his palm flat against it with fingers of a hand just touching the floor. He is the size of giants and here Aria stands before him, dripping.

The heat of the day makes the sensation pleasant - the cool seawater saturated into her dress poses as armour from the sun. A buzz of flies surrounds her, and she flinches away from their tiny bodies. Their attraction to her damp cotton pushes her forward, determined to be in a place that they are not. Thoughts of the boat flash across her mind. He would be worried, but it would be worth it.

She walks toward the hand; it is taller than she is. The man stares down on her, his brows tied together and his lips a limestone sneer. There is something disorientating about a statue, Aria had always thought so. Yet another reason to make haste finding her way in.

The tale that led her here was a short one. A cabin girl, a human girl, had told her of what they kept inside. A book. It exists in legend, but its use is unknown. Regardless, anything protected this way must be worth something. A legendary, rare book was all Aria had needed to hear to make her feel the urge to retrieve it. *For Jack.*

Ergo, here she is. She has dressed in white cotton, swum to the shore and worn shoes as per the instruction of the fable. Now she must find the door. She takes another look into the eyes of the stone man. He doubts her ability to complete this quest. He would give her no insight. Tapping his knuckle, she wills him to move.

And to her surprise, he does. The large hand shifts with an ancient delay, dust and pebbles falling and revealing an opening below it. A smile grows on her face, and she glimpses at his once more. There has been no change, but still she says, "Thank you."

Once she is inside, the door slams shut, sealing her inside. Her stomach flips as the room is plunged into darkness. The moment it is closed, the wet fabric is a hindrance. Inside these stone walls, the cold takes refuge. It is colder still from the realisation that she is trapped and alone. She closes her eyes and takes a deep breath.

"You're fine," she mutters to herself. It matters not if it is true, but that she believes it.

She takes a hesitant step. The click of her heel against the stone echoes in the space, bouncing off the high ceilings and cutting through the silence. She freezes, trying to listen for any approach.

She does not dare move again until her eyes adjust to the darkness. It is not as bad as she'd originally believed, slits of light struggle through thin cracks in the ceiling, forcing at least something into the space.

The room is now more than temporary blindness and she cannot see a sign of anything changing, or anyone approaching. No, but what she does see is distracting enough. Most of the area is bare. To her eyes, grey rock, dry and cold to touch, unkempt and as natural as a structure of stone can be. But the wall in front of her ignites her hope and kills it in the same moment.

Books line shelves of boulder, hundreds and hundreds of them, stretching for metres both upwards and out. They are ugly, old, and waterlogged. Maybe one of them is *the* book?

She thinks on her vague instruction. That cabin girl had given her nothing for when she got inside. Touching the books doesn't seem appropriate, it could not be that easy. She would have to improvise.

Okay.

She takes a deep breath before speaking, gathering her

nerves.

"Hello?" she calls into the empty space. Again, the noise bounces off the walls, and they sing to her.

She steps forward, turns and tries again. "Hello?"

Her voice is the only response she is given.

Aria sighs. Her choices seem limited. Look for a way out or touch the books.

Facing toward the entrance, she cannot even see the partition. Easy decision.

Returning to face the wall, her heart catches in her chest.

"Oh, Marie," she exclaims. But Marie isn't a person, Marie is a god. And she is not standing in front of Aria.

An arch has appeared, where there certainly had not been one before, carved into the bookshelf. It is still dark, but she can determine the figure of a man in the space. He steps forward and she hovers her hand over the dagger tied to her thigh. She is smart enough to have brought it, but not skilled enough to know how to use it.

Still, she scans him, looking for any sign that he might hurt her. She is naïve enough to think that he doesn't seem the type.

He does not move or speak. Just stares at her without curiosity.

"Good morning sir." It never hurts to be polite.

He says nothing, but the corners of his mouth twitch. She feels the seed of irritation plant itself in her. If he is going to stand there he could at least show her the courtesy of clear intention.

"I'm looking for a book." Impatience will not aid her.

"Yes." His lips part and the word falls out. It does not echo.

She has every right to be irritated.

"Can you help me?" she says.

"Why else would I be standing here?"

She takes a step toward him and watches as his mouth turns upwards. It is not an encouraging smile. It is made of lips that stick to teeth, and wrinkles that are more often seen on grimaces.

"Who are you? Should I be afraid?" Her hand returns to her thigh.

"Are you afraid?" Those words hold a gravity. They drop to the ground, and as soon as they land, the dark ink of them spreads throughout the space, painting ghosts in the dark.

She tenses her jaw, closes her eyes to dispel the enchantment, yet says nothing. *You are fine.* It matters not if it is true, only that she believes it.

The smile returns to his face and they are in an empty cave once again. In contrast to the prior moment, it seemed almost kinder.

"I'm here to help. You're not used to doing things alone now, are you?" he says.

Though it could have been an affable remark, it is presented as a jab. It permeates her growing distaste with this interaction. She stays silent.

"You are very good at that," he speaks again. "You're not very forthcoming, are you?" Another indignity. It isn't often quests are halted by cutting remarks in lieu of swords.

"Did I come here to be insulted?"

"I don't know *miss*. Did you?" The way he exaggerates the word. He knows that title in itself is an affront to her family name.

So, he knows her secrets. That makes her more uncomfortable than perhaps it should.

"I came for a book. The book," she says.

"Yet, you do not touch *the* books." His eyes shift to the wall around him, and hers follow.

Is that what is expected of her?

"I thought you were here to help me find it?" she hisses.

"And what is it?"

"The book. Where is the book?"

"What makes a book, *the* book?" he asks. That is a fair question and she should not resent him for it, still she does. He is the little man who lives in a cave, he is supposed to know the answer.

"I don't know," she mutters.

"Then you expect too much of me." He does not move to leave, in fact he stays as still as he had been throughout the entirety of their conversation. There must be something that she is missing.

"I am looking for the book that they all come here to find," she tries again.

"No one else has come here."

With his words her mind clears, this avenue proving fruitless. It seems as if her prior option is still her only one.

She sighs. The hairs of her arms and legs stand straight, and the cold pierces through her as if trying to remind her where she is. Alone, in a cave, with no way out. She walks toward a stone shelf, keeping her eyes on the little man as she does. His follow her also, and his smile widens the closer she gets. It unnerves her, but at least something she's doing is having some effect.

Reaching her hand out to the shelf she fingers the air until her hand rests on the woven fabric of a spine. She removes it from its place and opens it randomly. She flicks her gaze to the page, and then back to him. It is impossible to make sense of the text with her brief glances, but she doesn't trust him enough to look away.

After a handful of seconds of her attention, she realises the book is not in any language that she understands, so she returns it and retrieves another, eyes still fixed on her company. She repeats her vague analysis - this one was in Standard. She reads each word one by one, flicking her eyes back to his face after each. How. Do. You. Expect. To. Learn. Anything. This. Way.

She has barely read the final word, when she hears a laugh cut through the silence. This time it booms, and the walls are laughing, the pages are laughing. She can feel the book she holds shake from its amusement, the breath of the laughter on her face. Immediately, she drops it, her stare returning to the strange figure in the doorway.

More than one reaction feels natural in that moment, she wants to throw the books at him, she wants to back away, she wants to leave. But, she does none of the above.

Dropping to a crouch, she picks up the discarded manuscript. His laughter has ceased, and the room has returned to its lifelessness. Without reaction, she places the book back upon the shelf, watching the man, proving that he did not provoke fear.

"Not the trustworthy type, are we?" he finally speaks again.

"You've given me no reason to trust you." Her words do not sound as confident as she had meant them and she bites the insides of her cheeks, trying not to think about how the walls are getting smaller or how frustrated tears are beginning to sting behind her eyes.

A smirk appears and he watches her, before he nods. "Follow me."

"What?"

He has disappeared through the dark arch already.

For a second too long, hesitation keeps her on the spot, but she clears her mind, and follows.

What little light she had disappears as soon as she crosses through the threshold between rooms. It would have been alarming if she couldn't see a torch ahead, and the silhouette of the little man. She runs to try and catch up, deliberately ignoring the walls that lock her in and take her deeper into the cliff face. She can see nothing anyway, only make out the dim light of his flame.

It is harder than she thinks to reach him. It seems as if he'd travelled metres in the brief seconds she had lingered.

"Perhaps you could have waited?" She does not know for what reason she speaks. Maybe the silence unnerves her more than she cares to admit.

"Perhaps you could not have tarried?" His remark is welcome, and even teases the corners of her lips.

"How far does this hallway stretch?" she asks.

He stops dead and turns to her. She takes an involuntary step back, she had been closer than was sensible.

Predictably, he smiles at her discomfort. "Why don't you light a torch? Maybe one of these books is *the* book?"

For a moment, she does not understand. But following his gaze, she sees the light from the fire he holds illuminating dozens more titles listlessly arranged into shelves dug into the walls. At the edges of the circle of light they fade into indistinction.

As fascinating as the trick is, the book she was looking for was not among these, of that she was sure. Fairly sure.

"They are not." This time her voice does not shake and her resolve bolsters her.

The little man catches her gaze and keeps it. The light dims, and she begs her breath to quieten. To let him intimidate her is a weakness she cannot allow. He cocks his head, and that smile grows. Before she knows what's happening, he blows out his torch, pushing them back under the blanket of the dark.

It is as if she can taste it. Bitter and concentrated, it stings and sticks, choking her as it invades her lungs. It is thick, viscous, her mouth and throat are coated. It spreads over her face, quite literally blinding her. She wants to scream, but it is impossible around the intrusion.

Then she is coughing. Her chest heaves as her body tries to expel the alien substance.

"Princess?"

She gasps for air as her eyes snap open. Her body is no longer laboured with whatever has befallen her a second before. Her hands fumble over her person, searching for it, but all she finds is damp cloth. Even her lungs seem unaffected.

There is little time to think on that because they are no longer in that tunnel. Instead, a library of legend surrounds her. Nothing can compare to it. The room is built on books. They are found on every surface, in piles on the floor, blue, reds, golds and silvers. All pristine and placed with the intricacies of attention. It is huge, shelves block her from seeing the sheer magnitude of it from where she stands, but she searches for as far as she is able. Candles hang from every wall, the little that isn't cloth and paper is marble, gold or carpeting.

And she is shoeless.

It is only after she takes this in that she recognises what he has said. *Princess*.

"How do you know me?" There is no point in denying it, he is sure in his claim. With the use of her voice, she coughs again, only once. She catches something in her hand. It sticks her fingers to her palm as she opens it. *Ink*.

"Shouldn't everyone know you?"

Her head snaps back to him, her hand scraping across her front, mixing with the water and staining the white. She internally growls.

"Where is the book?" Her eyes are wide as she appeals for him to be honest with her. With this reveal, she just wants to find what she needs and leave. That secret is her armour, and he has stripped her of it. She is vulnerable.

He points to a door in front of her, a breath-taking mix of dark wood, carving and golden locks. Ominous in appearance, it is the natural choice for the way forward. Her sigh is confirmation of her understanding.

"How do I get through?" There is little hope in this question.

"You need to tell it why you're here," he says, surprising her.

"To get the book?"

Immediately, a clang resonates through her ears and throughout her head. A scream leaves her lips as the noise echoes. As soon as silence falls, her eyes rest on that irritating smirk.

"That much is obvious. Do you think anyone ventures in here to say hello?" he says.

She wants to highlight his contradiction, to scream at him, this door, and the room for enjoying her torture. But she does not, the weight of dread becoming known to her.

"I am here to procure a magical item to which I can gift to the love of my life. He has showered me with his time, his affections and his gifts for all the years that I have known him, and I want to be able to give him something that may possibly live up to all that he has given me in the past."

It is silent and she stares at the locks, willing them to move. Instead she is met with another clang that may have frightened her more than the first, her concentration violently broken by the sound.

"It knows when you're not being honest with it." The ever-present smugness drips from his voice.

"It is a door." The words escape through pressed lips.

"One last chance."

"What?"

"You heard me."

A thought comes then. "If I get this wrong, is there any way out?"

"How does one get their own intentions wrong?" he responds and the slit of his mouth shapes into a rounded antagonist.

She says nothing.

"Is this uncomfortable for you because you're a liar

Aria?" The way he stresses a name that doesn't belong to her is a weapon in itself.

She hears him open those lips to speak again, but she interjects, talking instead to the door. "For recompense. I am already promised to another. And I have known that for years. Maybe this will soften the blow."

There is a pause. It seems to be endless, but eventually one by one, the locks click open. It is a hypnotising sight, watching them all, the left side separating itself from that which it had previously boasted an unbreakable bond, splitting with no guarantee of reconnection. When they are finished, the door stays as it had been, it does not open for her.

She looks to the man for advice as to what to do, but it is as if he'd never existed. She stands alone in that grand room. She takes one final look, but when she looks too close, the colours run together, leaking into one another, and the walls are peeling at the limits of her vision.

She is on her own, and here is a door.

She pushes on the heavy dark wood and steps out into the forest. The sun filters through the trees, the smell of the ocean not too far away, the wind feeding through the curls of her hair, some of which are stuck to her chest.

An arm which she swears she had used to open the door cradles a deep red book that almost seems to glow. Though she can hear voices, familiar voices, coming from not too far away, she throws the pages open, curious as to what a book that had been worth so much inconvenience would include. Inside were pages upon pages of spells that promise money, time, and the part that piques her interest; *solutions.*

The voices are getting louder now.

"Aria!" Warm hands cup her shoulders and bring her body toward him. She pushes away, eager to give him her gift and to discover all the possibilities of what it might mean for them. Solutions. Perhaps she'd never have to tell him.

Thrusting it into his grasp, she exclaims, "Happy Birthday!"

"It's not my birthday."

Half of Jacks face turns up into a smile as he takes the book from her. She cannot explain why the smile causes a wave of unease to attach itself to her.

She shakes it off, she has spent too long in the dark. Jack says nothing as he flicks through the pages, she watches his face, holding her breath. He has to love it. He has to. With each new page, his smile evolves and shifts, until he lets out a scoff with a sense of achievement.

"Well, that was easier for me to procure than I expected." The words dress her with paranoia.

"What— What do you mean? Do you like it? Did you see —" A piercing whistle cuts her off and draws the attention of his crew toward where they stand.

"Time to go boys!" He holds up the red book like a beacon as he turns away. She waits a moment, to see if he will turn back, to see if he will address her at all.

Her pride wants her to say nothing, to let him walk away, but she cannot. "I don't understand." It isn't quite a call, but it is enough to make him pause.

"I don't need you anymore." His tone is matter of fact. He sighs. "I can't have you anymore."

"You— what? That book?" She tries to make sense of it in her head, to think of any time that he spoke of needing, or even wanting it.

"Thank you. Truly. Thank you for getting this for me, but we both know *we* couldn't last. We had a good time, and this book sets me on a new adventure," he pauses, "one I cannot take with you."

"So you're just going to leave me here?"

He says nothing, yet he still has the nerve to look guilty.

"I'm sorry," he finally presents.

And then he walks away, leaving her damp and desperate in the green. The words escape before she's given them licence, only a whisper offered to the air, "It was supposed to be you."

She feels the tears come, and that is the only feeling she can place. She tries to focus on her legs, to take a step, to do something.

It seems as if a herculean effort, but as soon as she moves, the grass shifts below her, and the wind disappears. Her bare foot falls on cold stone and again her sight is lost.

Nestled within her elbow is something, another book. A

familiar damp smell is unignorable and she glances down at her dress. Her eyes are beginning to harness the slivers of the light in the room, and from that she can tell it is no longer white. She recognises it to have remained sodden, but now almost freshly soaked, heavier. Her hair is weighted too and she shakes her head throwing around the smell of metal.

It is definitely a book. And in front of her is definitely the bookshelves she had seen upon first entry. When she turns around the rock moves, revealing the opening in which she'd entered.

"Aurea?" She hears the voice repeated endlessly, the worry woven into each syllable. That is the voice she knows.

She barely takes a step before she collides with him. Throwing her arms around him she lets the relief drop her into his hold. He ushers her out.

"Are you okay?" He studies her face, each feature he checks twice. "Your dress—" His shirt is now stained in black ink.

She breaks from his grasp, but he keeps one hand on her arm. She offers him the book, yet he ignores it. "What were you thinking?"

She says nothing, just offers it again, more forcibly than before. There is a hesitant, awkward edge to her movements. She wonders if he notices.

Taking the gift, he spins it in his hands, studying the stainless pale blue buckram. His face contorts into one of confusion.

"You went for a book? Aria, what happened in there, are you okay?"

She hesitates before she gives her answer. A flashback in a quarter of a second. *It was supposed to be you.*

"I am absolutely perfect," she says, allowing her eyes to shine and her grin to dazzle.

It matters not if it is true, but only that he believes it.

"Sometimes when the world gets too dark, it's okay to want something warm to hold onto. Here's something fluffy to warm the cockles of your heart."

LUCY ROSE
Twitter @lucyrosecreates

Award-winning writer and director based in the North of England. Lover of Charity Shop Books, Folkore and Copious Tea Drinking.

The Orange Seller

MY CHILDHOOD, LIKE MOST, was wrapped in the love of my parents. They shielded me from the plight of adulthood by reading me bedtime stories about Princes and Princesses. They would fall in love, their estates would merge, and their love would be unending. Their people would love them in return, almost as much as they loved each other.

One story in particular always seemed to stay with me. How a prince fell in love with a common girl and she became a princess. From poverty to riches.

One night, I asked when I would fall in love.

Mother's decision to stop reading such stories left a space that's never been filled. At such a young age, I couldn't understand why there was no answer to such a simple question.

I would later learn it was because I was never meant to fall in love.

* * *

The air had gone sparse and left me breathless.

The thick scent of honeysuckle was strong on the breeze, and the sun's lazy rays gave everything a wishful haze. Summer was taking hold of my kingdom, from the sweeping fields and meadows of the north, to the marketplace that sat, ever shifting and ever alive, at the base of the hill. Sat gilded and showered with expensive riches and unnecessary embellishment at the highest point was my family home. Castle De Clarone.

None of these things, however, held my interest today. Only *she* did.

The girl before me beheld a most precious beauty. More so than any gods could wish upon their fairest muses, or even themselves. A beauty that fell past her skin and dripped into her soul. Her dark olive flesh radiated a dark honey-like warmth and beneath a simple shirt and a worker's hat, hair escaped like wildflowers under a garden stone.

Striking sapphire eyes watched passers-by warmly as she manned her stall — until they met mine. *There*, they held me. Our glances had caught one another in a web.

I stepped closer, placing my hands upon the scratched wood of her stall, until I could see the gold passing between the blue in her eyes.

Even the most potent of love elixirs couldn't cast such an enchantment.

"Good morning." The words seemed to tumble from my lips without any grace. This wasn't how I was raised to behave. My simple awe was comparable to that of a child seeing a mythic creature. She was something of fairy tales.

"What can I do for you?" There was a blush on her cheeks and, upon a closer glance, dimples resting either side of her lips when she spoke.

Behind me, one of my guards followed closely, hovering only mere feet away. With a glance over my shoulder, I noted his pensive stare: a warning to move on. I ignored it, finding myself turning back to the woman.

"A name?" I asked, unsure if my words bore any meaning to her. Clarity was escaping me in every sense. Her raised eyebrow was question enough. "Please give me a name or silence me forever," I faltered. She cocked her head and smiled.

"There's a lot in a name. Maybe I shouldn't," she teased, somewhat bashful on account of my clear intrigue, but enjoying it. "Especially not with a palace guard so close by," she continued. She pointed at me and started a guessing game. "A dignitary. Or a criminal. Perhaps you're out on furlough. I suppose I would need a name from you to be able to tell." Her tone was inviting and friendly. I felt the guard's breath on my neck and turned to glare.

"Would you step back? You need not be so close," I cautioned. He nodded and retreated. I returned my attention to the woman, bewitched by the way her eyes gleamed with something close to magic.

A forced smile cut my face, knowing my name would mean more to her than any name should. "Ameile De

Clarone."

"Your majesty," she gasped. Those lovely eyes dropped to her feet, as she bowed her head to me — a sudden panic had grasped her. All her playful regard dissolved into fear. "My name is Orelia."

"You need not bow to me," I tilted my head gracefully and returned my gaze to her. Lifting a hand to her, she flinched, and for a moment I cursed whoever may have touched her before. I placed two fingers under her chin and lifted until her eyes met mine again. I sensed her fear drip away as a tender smile was summoned to her lips.

"Princess Ameile," the guard coughed.

I pulled my hand away from Orelia's soft skin, swearing to myself it would not be the last time I felt that silk touch. My cheeks were crimson, and my heart racing, but I knew what my guard's few words were telling me.

My hours of escape had ended, but with that warning I snatched a ripe orange to remember her by.

* * *

In the days that passed, I would look from my window out to the market, wondering if Orelia was sitting idly by her stall and thinking of me. In the mornings, it was the worst, and I would catch my drifting thoughts like boats untethered, scrambling to bring myself back under order.

While her eyes sparkled in my memory, I could not shake

a suspicion that some spell had been cast, some hex, to keep my attention on a girl in the market I'd met only once.

Why her?

A moment of weakness had led to my confession to my Mother, the Queen. I described the flutter in my chest, and the way my mind fell back to her eyes whenever mine closed. I questioned love like nothing else.

And while it was obvious any sign of my affections being turned towards someone of lowly stature would be met with ambivalence, nothing could have prepared me for the rejection they posed to me.

"It's the summer heat," Mother scolded as she rose from her polished throne and started towards me. She rested her chilled fingers on my forehead and washed me with a grave look of concern.

"I'm serious," I whispered, pulling her hand away from me.

"She's been carried away with the bees, George," Mother fussed as she returned to my father's side.

"No more of this madness." Father rarely spoke, and when he did, it was often to change the subject. His dismissiveness was nothing if not consistent, but it riled me all the same.

Even in that bleak moment of hoping that Mother and Father would understand, Orelia was all I could think of. She was always lodged in my mind, like a ship's anchor being tethered to the seabed.

The throne room was gilded with all kinds of needless riches. Slabs of slate rested in monotonous patterns and tired but elegant tapestries hung from the walls. Two golden thrones sat at the top of the room, covered in intricate and delicate patterns. I used to trace my fingers through the grooves as a child, knowing I'd one day comfortably sit there.

The King and Queen both took up a seat with ferocious posture and stared down on me as I knelt on the step before them.

"Please, Father," I called, breaking what they expected to be the silence at the end of the conversation. "I see her in the constellations of stars, and in the brush strokes of paintings. All I ask is for permission to act on my heart," I pleaded, knowing that those beauties combined couldn't equal hers.

"Enough!" Father's voice echoed.

"Am I not to be loved?" I asked, letting my fears and questions slip past my lips. The silence my strength had held all these years had buckled. The question hung in the air and my father's stare withstanding its weight. Mother's eyes dropped away from mine, and for a moment I heard her heart say *no, my daughter. You are not.*

That evening, as summer rain fell from sky to earth, I watched the market lights from the top of the hill, knowing their warmth couldn't reach me. Mother sent me a plate of pears as a peace offering, but I knew there was no way I could eat. My stomach, along with the rest of me, was not mine anymore.

It belonged to the market girl.

* * *

While the moon was overhead, the cold light came in through my curtains in beams to wake me from my slumber. I felt how empty my bed was. My room was cold and blue, but nothing like the blue in her eyes. This was not an ocean sapphire - it was frostbitten hue of cobalt. Unkind and lonely.

Finally, my want to sleep and have this day be over was lost to my want to start another. I suspect the guards knew my plan — one too many conveniently unlocked doorways and unmanned corridors — so I dressed in my darkest of day-clothes and made my way through the castle's halls. The gates to the gardens were ajar, leaving me with a clear pathway to the palace walls that overlooked the market.

My breath caught on the chilled evening air as I scaled the vines up the white-stone bricks.

The mud from the hillside sullied my clothes, and the market was long-since closed by the time I got there, but there was nothing left for me to go back to.

I couldn't leave until I saw her again.

Whatever magic she had ensnared me with either needed uncast, or I needed to see it through to its end. I owed myself this indulgence of love, if my life was to be absent of it forever after.

Daylight forced my eyes open. No longer was the sun warm and lazy, now it was strained and crisp on my eyelids.

Sounds of carts on cobbles brought me to consciousness, and the smell of cooked fruits and baker's bread filled my wanting lungs. My back, arched from sleeping against a wall by the market stall, ached like nothing else, and my heart sank as I saw the stall, still vacant.

I walked up to the kiosk, tracing my finger against the empty wooden trays, from which I had once stolen an orange with a smile.

"She'll be back tomorrow," the woman from the next stall over said, smiling to me as she set up her cart. "Poor girl came down with something rotten."

"Where is she?" I asked. As the woman started giving me directions, I scorned myself for not bringing any way to record them and had to hope that my memory was as clear as my goal.

Her cottage sat on the outskirts of the kingdom, a modest build of brick and log. It was drenched in the dim-orange hue of sunrise.

The country lane lead me to the front door, and as I raised my hand to knock, I hesitated. We had only met once, a few days ago. Would she even remember our meeting?

Did I impact her the way she did me? The extent of my one-sided affair was embarrassing to face, especially with the subject of my affections so close.

Before either my shame won out, or my hope enveloped me, the choice was taken from me.

The door swung open, and there she stood.

By the lights, she had the kindest face I'd ever had the grace of beholding.

"Princess-"

"I missed you at the market," I blurted out. A smile snaked her sweet lips, and I allowed hope to take me. "I missed you everywhere."

She stepped past me, not saying a word. She gave only a glance over her shoulder, inviting me to follow. We crossed the garden path, into an orange orchard the scale of which I was familiar with — even from the castle, you could see the luscious fruits, dotted with shining sunlight-auburns from on high. The trees glowed in the early light, and the fruit shimmered with a colour of which I fear I'd never see the equal of.

"No guard?" she asked.

I shook my head. "The King and Queen are not happy with me. Nor you."

"Me?" She turned, the look of insult on her face turning to a playful smile. "Whatever did I do?"

I only had one answer. "You stole my heart. Never could I settle for a marriage arranged for me, not now."

"You've known me a day."

"I've known you a lifetime," I corrected. "I've only just met you, Orelia. There's a difference."

She stopped under a tree; the pottering shadows cascaded across her face in serene patterns. Her cheeks flushed an elegant ruby and then straightened as she pushed the smile off her face. Resting herself on the ground, her back to the bark, she patted the ground next to her.

I joined her in an instant. Her bare feet tapped against my muddied shoes, which I had taken from my father's childhood collection. Where else was a Princess to find shoes that would last a hillside?

She produced an orange, and held it out to me, but as I went to accept it, she snatched it back, laughing softly. *Gods, her laugh is infectious.* She peeled back the orange skin and set free the sweetest aroma.

"You've not yet paid for the last one," she smiled. "Did you think I wouldn't see you snatch away one of my oranges?"

"I've no money to pay," I urged.

She scoffed and took a segment to her lips. She spoke through as she chewed, her mouth swollen and full and making me laugh at her silliness. "You're the Princess, *Princess.*"

"I'd give it up," I whispered. "Given the right..."

She met my eyes, looking for the end of that sentence. "The right what?"

"Motivation."

I leaned forwards, and she smiled, pushing an orange segment to my lips. But just as I was to taste the sweet juice, she stood and bounded away, leaving me to take a bite, alone.

I could have chased her forever, I thought as I stood, following her deeper into the orchard.

* * *

Orelia was a woman built with warmth and compassion. She had decorated her cottage with all kinds of curiosities. On her mantel piece sat several wood carvings of birds, and there were old books lining every open surface. She told me that her friend owned a bookshop, and anything that became cheap enough for a market seller to buy, he'd bring it to her. She had books on anything and everything; ship building, the conservation of certain wild creatures, historical texts on far-off lands. She'd read every single one of them.

I thought of my room, in the castle. By comparison it was so bare, and hardly any of the things in there belonged to me at all. They were brought in by others, posed as gifts, but they failed in their purpose to make me feel at home.

This home, however, was unmistakably Orelia's. Her wares were old and tattered, but so thoroughly loved. Chairs with holes in them, and tables with rings where tea had spilled and dried.

We had spent the day picking oranges, and Orelia had

admitted her lie, she was not ill. She simply felt the need to take time alone. Any guilt I may have felt for stepping into that time was short-lived; she invited me in with wide arms.

She cooked us a pie, made with fruit from her orchard that was too soft to sell, and we ate together. On a tiny wooden table, in a cluttered kitchen, at the front of a cottage, at the base of the town.

I tried to picture my mother, or, laughably, my father in this place. They would call it cramped or complain of the smell of citrus overwhelming them. Anything different to their expectations was a disappointment - no surprises would ever bring them joy.

Maybe that's why they reject me? I asked for love, but they gave me tradition.

The midday sun baked us through the window pane while we ate, and she was lined with a halo of sunlight. The tight curls in her brown hair shone and her dark skin seemed to take on a shade of gold. Those striking eyes glistened when she smiled, and her dimples marked her beauty as something to behold. For that day, we hid from the world, together, under a glowing sun and surrounded by the smell of sweet fruits.

"I never want to leave," I heard myself say, breaking the comfortable silence between us. She offered me her hand, and a warm smile. Her skin was just as soft as I remembered.

"You don't have to."

It sounded like such a small offer when she said it,

but there were such enormous consequences to what she suggested. I felt myself pull my hand back. "I do," I said. "The King and Queen will be awaiting their daughter, Orelia. There is nowhere to hide from them.'

"One night," she said, standing. "Spend tonight with me, Princess?"

How was I to resist?

We lay on the stone floor by the hearth and covered our flesh in cinders as we entwined our fingers. The fire embers glowed amidst the shadows around us, but even in the obscure ebbing light, I couldn't be drawn to a more radiant spark than her. I held on for my life and breath as the reflection of the dying fire painted her blue eyes gold.

"Why must you go?" she asked me, whispering into the silence. Her lips, which I watched ardently, barely moved. Part of me thought she was maybe worried she would scare me away if she spoke too loud. But fear had very little to do with it anymore.

We hadn't made it far from the kitchen. The hearth was lit, and the night sky outside had blossomed into stars and moonlit secrets hours ago. Blankets and cushions kept our flesh from the chilled stone as we bundled together.

All the fires in the land could not compare to the heat of her breath.

"They expect me to." It was the only answer I had, and even as I said it, I knew how it sounded. It sounded weak.

Self-destructive. Happy to accept a cruel fate that need not belong to me.

She looked up to me and didn't bother to say another word. In truth, there was very little need for her to speak; the flutter of her eyelids and the quiver of her lips told me everything.

I put my fingers to her chin, as I had that first day in the market, and lifted until her lips met mine. Our first kiss was slow, filling the air with tension. The glowing embers of the hearth's fire held us.

Her hand in my hair. My smile on her kiss.

I needed her like the tides need the moon to do the gods will. I needed her more than crops need the sunlight to survive until harvest.

I needed her.

* * *

My mother, in my childhood, would read me stories of Princes and Princesses who would fall in love.

One night, after reading a story of a scullery maid becoming a princess, I asked when I would fall in love.

Her decision to stop reading such stories left me without hope for such a love to consume me. At such a young age, I couldn't understand why there was no answer to such a simple question.

I would later learn it was because I was never meant to

fall in love. I was never meant to give up the hilltop castle. I was never meant to meet her, and it was made clear that she would not be welcome as royalty.

So, instead of taking Orelia with me, I went with her. From riches to rags. From log fires to warm breath. From hilltop to orchard.

In a heartbeat and without condition, I gave up the crown.

"I wanted it to represent the people who feel and think differently, who don't con-form to the normal, who think outside the box."

R.W. STAINCLIFFE
Twitter @rstaincliffe1

Born in Newcastle, studied film and television at Northumbria University, worked across multiple film & TV productions, now moving into teaching. Loves football, proudly gay man.

The Tree

THERE WAS ONCE A LITTLE BOY who lived in the shadow of a tree. But this wasn't just any ordinary tree. Sitting atop a hill, with a sheer cliff drop on one side, its branches were as thick as an elephant's trunk and its leaves delighted in the purest green, still that wasn't what made this tree special. From each of its leaves sprouted a vine and these vines connected to the other vines around it, coming together to form layer after layer after layer. Underneath the vines, hanging peacefully from the branches, seven small shapes could be seen. No one knew what they were, how they got there or even why, but they had become the stuff of legend.

Some said each one formed an object that gave the collector ultimate power. Others said they formed a weapon so powerful that the Kings had ordered them to be destroyed, but the task proved impossible, so they were broken and placed where no one would ever reach them. And the rest said it was all a load of mumbo jumbo and they had better things to be doing with their lives.

Not the Little Boy. Every day he stared out his window; longing, wondering, wanting to know. Every time he and his mother would leave the house to go to the market, he would say to her, "Mother, one day I will know what's up there."

She would just roll her eyes, ruffle his hair and say, "Of course dear."

However, the Little Boy was not the only one who eyed the tree. Peasants, soldiers, even noblemen travelled from far and wide to try and climb it. As many as ten men could be seen climbing at any one time and it wouldn't be long before ten men were walking away empty handed, unable to even get close to the first shape.

The Little Boy watched men walk up the hill day after day proud as punch, but leave with their tail between their legs, having paid his father for the pleasure of doing so.

The rules were simple. A Challenger got one go. They wrote their name in the 'Book of Challengers' and signed with blood, thus binding them to the rule of the tree. Each Challenger had from sunrise to sunset to complete their quest. If they did not return to the ground of their own accord, the tree would see to it. If a Challenger for any reason called out 'I yield', they would be returned to the ground gently by the tree. If a Challenger fell and both feet hit the ground they would also relinquish their challenge. They were allowed to use any means necessary to try and climb the tree but if any harm came to the tree, the Challenger would not live a second after. Thankfully, this had never happened - yet.

The Little Boy studied each and every one, waiting

to see what it would be that got them. Often it was their own stupidity. Many became trapped in the vines, having to squeal 'I yield' before scurrying away. Others simply fell from the branches. Some came armed with concoctions created with the specific purpose of beating the tree. Some turned to magic, a strength elixir was as regularly seen on a Challenger as a pint would be on a drunkard. Others turned to machinery, elaborate and sometimes frankly ridiculous creations that often hindered the wearer.

Once nightfall had set in and the tree had remained unconquered the Little Boy lay down in bed as his father came in to say goodnight.

"Father, when will I be ready to climb the tree?"

The Little Boy's Father laughed and ruffled his hair.

"One day, when you're big and strong."

He plants a kiss on the Little Boy's head before closing the door. The Little Boy rolls over and drifts off to the same dream, sitting atop the tree as the sun rises, the eyes of the world upon him.

The following day was the same, and the next day and the next. Challengers would come, fail and leave – the Tree unmoved, unconquerable.

Then one afternoon, whilst returning from the market with his mother, the Little Boy noticed something odd. All the Challengers were climbing up the same part of the tree. He wondered whether to question Mother about it, because there must be a reason they're all there although no one had ever succeeded. Instead he made a mental note to study that part of the tree extra hard when he returned home.

The next day, sat on the roof, the Little Boy noticed something else. All of the Challengers were men. Smart men, small men, thin men, thick men, noblemen, strong men, but all men that would eventually fail.

The Little Boy thought this might just be coincidence, so he made sure to study the Challengers closely the next day. Again, all who came were men and all went to the same part of the tree. Maybe, the Little Boy thought, you needed to not be a man and not climb that part of the tree to win. But he would only ever get one go – did he really want to use it now?

He could climb, proven by his current position, but could he climb all that way? The tree dwarfed everything around it, its top could be seen for miles and miles around. It would be a colossal feat for a grown man to climb that high, never mind a small Boy. He decided he was not ready but he would not wait until he was a man. He decided that on his thirteenth birthday he would climb the tree.

For the years that followed, the Little Boy trained intensively. He practised climbing three hours every day. He made himself 'vines' out of anything he could find and practised manipulating them to do what he wanted, to help, not hinder him. He ran along the cliff above every morning, looking at the untouched part of the tree, plotting his course. He ate well, even when he didn't feel like doing so, he knew he would need everything that was given to him. He made notes on those that got the furthest up the tree, what they did good and what caused them to fail.

One day when the Little Boy was no longer little, he sat in his room watching out the window as he usually did. He looked to his left and saw the sun very nearly disappear behind the cliff, the signal to give up and yield. Soon the air was filled with the frustrated cries of 'I yield' and one by one they were lowered down to the ground. The Boy's Father scratched off their names. In a moment his face suddenly changed, an expression the Boy had never seen before. He looked up and saw a man still trying to climb.

"Father," the Boy called, getting his attention. "He's up there."

The Boy's Father's eyes widened in terror.

"Yield you fool!" he screamed, his voice bouncing around the clifftops, the other Challengers turning to see what all the fuss was about.

"Never!" the Man called back.

The Man turned and continued to climb, his arms aching, his legs shaking with pain, the progress slow.

The Boy hurried downstairs to his Father's side.

"Go back inside," his Father said.

"Father," the Boy protested.

"Son, you don't want to see this."

But it was too late. The sun dropped behind the cliff as a blood curdling scream echoed through the sky. The vine was holding the man upside down by his ankle.

"Son, close your eyes."

"Father..."

"Son, just..."

Another vine raced towards the man. The Boy's father grabbed his head and pushed it into his chest, trying to stop him seeing, but it was too late. The Boy witnessed the vine rip through the man's neck like a knife through butter, head and body apart as they fell into the darkness below. The Boy's dream changed that night. He was no longer sat atop the tree; he was dangling over the darkness – vines racing towards him.

The tree remained untouched for months after, the Boy's father refusing to let anyone near it, the Boy no longer preparing to climb it. However, with no other income he soon had to waive his guilt and let those that were still willing take on the tree.

The Boy needed to entertain himself, keep the thoughts of the man out of his head. He soon decided that he had to climb the tree, he had to conquer it to save anyone else from perishing.

He trained twice as hard, for longer. From sunrise to sunset he trained and trained and trained. He no longer needed to study what the others did. He was going to do this his way.

The day of his thirteenth birthday arrived. The Boy was ready. He woke before sunrise and made his way to the tree.

He opened the book and signed it before his father could stop him. The tree swayed in the wind, the vines seemingly more menacing up close and personal. He stood waiting, no contraptions, no potions, just himself and his plan waiting to go. His eyes were fixated on the cliff, as soon as the sun touched it the tree would be fair game. He knew it wouldn't be long. He didn't turn around and look, he kept focused. He could feel the air beginning to warm, the faintest sliver of sunlight touched the clifftop just as the Boy's Father emerged. He looked on in horror as the Boy set off, gently easing himself onto the first vine. He ran over to the book to see the signature and the blood mark. He knew that there was nothing he could do.

"Be careful," he muttered, "come home."

The Boy took a moment to compose himself making sure his grip was steadfast. He looked up at the imposing sight, the mangle of vines as far as his eyes could see, yet he felt calm, he felt ready. He'd waited for this moment patiently, he'd studied, he'd learned.

He could hear the mumblings of the gathering crowd, the other Challengers arriving to see a boy there ahead of them. He knew he had to move, they would interfere, they wouldn't understand.

The Boy started to move not up but along, the vines below becoming leafy stepping stones, allowing him to easily travel across. There was no struggle, no grappling, the progress was measured, his movements slow and methodical.

Soon, he was out of sight of the other Challengers, he was alone – only the tree for the company. He steadied himself once more, taking a moment to catch his breath, go over the plan once more. You see from all his studying; the Boy had noticed something interesting. The tree was a living being, for all a curious and imposing one, which didn't like to be treated harshly. That's why the rule was in place about causing it harm. The ham fisted, lead footed men would thrash and grab and stomp and kick and pull and stretch and the more they did so, the more the tree resisted. The angry, red faced men were always the ones who would yield – several vines wrapped around an ankle, an arm, a neck. He had to be kind, be gentle. Even when he felt panicked, in trouble, he knew he had to stay calm and gentle. If he did that, then maybe the tree would help him.

So, as he began to climb he made sure he was as gentle as possible – not grabbing, not pulling, not causing harm. Soon he found his progress was swifter, much swifter. Instead of dropping when he put his weight on them, the vines began to hold firm, almost pushing him up. He looked into the blue sky, seeing the sun was clear above the horizon. He was making steady progress but he needed to be quicker, there was still a long way to go, and he had to get back down as well.

A cry of 'I yield' snapped the Boy back to. He started the climb again, the vines strong underfoot – he was winning the tree over, he could feel it. He could feel himself finding gaps in the vines a lot easier, there seemed to be less of them now and through one of these gaps he saw it, a shape hanging from the branch. He wasn't sure if the rumours were true because he wasn't convinced anyone had gotten up high enough to see them before. He'd tried during his cliff top runs to spy them but he had never seen clearly enough to know for sure. Now he did.

He parted the vines in front of him and using his legs to pressure the vines by his knees, he swung onto the massive branch in front of him. Gingerly peeling off the greenery, the Boy stood up on the branch, easily three steps each side before the sheer drop, before edging slowly towards the small object hanging at its edge. The closer he got, the more he could make out its shape.

It looked like a set of small arms, toy like, with small round pieces of wood sticking out of the top. The Boy, now within arm's reach, went to grab it, but just as soon as it was there it wasn't anymore. He couldn't believe it.

He turned around and to his surprise the arm was hanging at the other end of the branch, on the opposite side of the tree. The Boy quickly shuffled along, watching each and every footstep as he did so, until he was within arms reach once again.

He reached out but like before the arm disappeared. The Boy turned around and to his annoyance it was now back over the other side of the tree.

He stood, contemplating. This was a part he couldn't

have studied for, this time he would have to think on his feet.

He went over the rules; he went over *his* rules. Be kind, be gentle, don't hurt it, don't act like them below. He'd been kind so far, he'd been so gentle when at times he wanted to push and grab and claw, he hadn't hurt it, he'd done everything different to the others, the men below. Then it hit him. He'd grabbed. He'd tried to take it without permission.

But how did he get permission? Could he talk to the tree? It was a living thing after all, surely it could hear him? He made his way to the other side of the tree and sat down just out of reach of the arms. He looked around at the tree, searching out for anything that might be considered an ear. He couldn't see anything so he sat for a moment.

What would he do if he wanted something from his Mother at the market, or off his Father before he went to bed? He let his legs swing, lolling down over the abyss below. Time ticked by, the Boys frustration grew because he just couldn't clear his mind, see through the fog. Then he heard it, a deep booming voice from another Challenger below.

"Please! Please let me go!" It begged. It did not let go because soon after the voice whimpered.

"I yield, I yield – let me go!"

As the Challenger was lowered to the ground, the Boy's mind cleared. He stood up, dusted himself down before turning and looking at the arms, drifting merrily in the gentle breeze. He cleared his throat and in his squeaky voice said.

"Hello, Mr or Mrs Tree, please, please may I have the arms hanging on this branch?"

An eternity seemed to pass by before the arms dropped and fell. Tentatively, the Boy moved forward towards them, waiting for them to disappear. They didn't. He gathered them up, looking them over once or twice before putting them in his trouser pocket.

"Thank you."

He moved back towards the vines, preparing to climb once more, but he decided he might ask one more favour of the tree.

"Hello, me again. Could you help me? Could you please show me the easiest way to the next object?"

Before he could even take another breath, a vine wrapped itself around his ankle and violently swung him out over the abyss. Holding onto his pocket, the Boy screamed, looking straight down into the darkness below. He tried to angle himself to see his house but he couldn't, the tree was just too big.

If he fell, his parents would only know when the sun set. He didn't want that. The words crossed his mind but as soon as they did, the vine didn't let go – it started pulling him higher, up the tree. He didn't appreciate being carried upside down but he did appreciate the help, the burning in his arms slowly dying away.

Soon he was facing the right way and standing on the next branch – in front of him two toylike legs, also with round wooden sticks poking out the top.

"Hello tree, thanks for your help. Could I please have the legs hanging on that branch there?"

Again the legs dropped onto the branch below, and he picked them up.

"Thanks," the Boy said, preparing himself for the sudden jerk that would come with the vine grabbing his legs but none came. He looked around, no vines were near him. The Boy considered, maybe he had asked too much this time? He was soon answered.

As he looked further, he saw what seemed to be small steps that had been carved into the trunk of the tree. He carefully approached them, putting his hands in the grooves. He pulled, making sure they were secure, not some trick of the light or a dummy. Satisfied, he started to climb, not noticing the vine wrap itself around his waist, a safety harness.

The climb was long, the burning returning to his arms and legs, but it was as if the grooves had been cut just for him. He managed to see the sun was now past it's peak, on the downward arc of its day, but no sooner had he clocked this was he at the next opening.

This time what awaited the Boy was a toy like body, four round wood sticks sticking out – exactly where arms and legs would attach. The body was muscular, very muscular –

unlike any man the Boy had ever seen. He again asked the tree to relinquish it and once again it did.

"Thanks," the Boy muttered as he joined the arms and legs to the body. He noticed a space where the head would be – the next object he thought.

He moved back towards the trunk but this time it was wrapped tight with vines, like a python around its prey, squeezing the life from it.

All of a sudden, the branch below the Boy gave way. He jumped and clung onto the nearest vine as he watched the heavy branch fall and continue, taking some of the vines with it. He could see the sun dangerously close to the horizon.

He may have been cunning enough but was he indeed ready for this challenge? Did he have the physical strength to deal with what the tree would throw at him? He was being tested now as he clung onto the vine, trying to hook his legs up for more support.

He hung for a moment, considering those words again, nowhere else to go. He noticed perhaps twenty metres below him, a net of sorts had formed. He looked down at it, it lined up perfectly with him. Could he make it? If he dropped would it take the impact? What would it do to him?

If it only caught him he would have lost valuable time, time he couldn't make back, yet if it catapulted him he would surely be faster? Was it worth it? He looks at the body and arms – he'd come so far, further than anyone ever had. He couldn't give up now.

With that thought he let go, leaving himself at the mercy of the tree. The wind whistled past his ears as he fell. He kept his eyes closed, he didn't want to see if he was going to miss – he would know soon enough. He thought of his family as he waited, particularly his Mother's smile. He soon had his answer. The vines pressed hard against his body, he could feel the pressure raw on his skin. He slowed almost to a stop, he thought he was going to break through but he didn't.

The Boy inhaled deeply as he was catapulted high into the sky and he couldn't help but scream as he barrelled straight into the tree, higher than before. He shook the leaves out of his hair as he noticed he'd landed on the next branch – the toylike head in his grasp.

He quickly fixed it in place on the body and waited. Nothing – the face was motionless. It was near dark now.

The Boy ran to the end of the branch, climbed onto the vines and looked up. He was twenty metres from the top. The sun had almost set. Could he make it? He was definitely going to try. Now he grabbed, now he pushed, now he pulled – desperate to complete the challenge. He couldn't come this far and fail, he just couldn't.

The vines started to weaken, dropping under his weight, wrapping themselves around him. He could feel them trying to get into his pocket, trying to take the body from him. The Boy grasped it tight in his hand. He could see a faint glow from the top of the tree. He craved it but the tree had had enough. The vines wrapped tighter and tighter around him, pulling him into the trunk. The sun was about to set, he knew what happened to those who didn't say the words. He had no option. As a vine wrapped itself around his throat – the Boy called out.

"I yield... I yield."

The vines stopped. The Boy looked as the sun dipped behind the horizon. He let out a sigh of relief, figure still in hand. They repositioned – carrying the Boy gracefully down to the ground arms outstretched, like the Messiah being brought down to Earth. The Boy could see the relief in his mother's eyes, his father holding onto her tightly. As his feet touched the ground, they enveloped him in love, arms wrapped around and bodies close. He could hear his father's heart pounding like never before, his mother's hands trembling. He was home, he was safe, and he had done the seemingly impossible.

He'd conquered the tree.

"A mermaid story had been swimming in my subconscious for some while, but when I started to write, she turned out to be a he, and the answer to a maritime mystery!"

P.J. RICHARDS
Twitter @P_J_Richards

P.J. Richards is a writer and artist living in Somerset, England, surrounded by the folklore, nature and history that inspires her work. When not weaving words, or ink and paint, she can be found living in castles, shooting her longbow.

Celeste

HE LIES ON THE SURFACE of the water for a moment, held by the air in his clothes, cradled by the gentle swell of the waves. Then he folds and rolls until his face turns towards the fathoms that draw him twirling deeper and deeper, past my stroking hands. Is there enough of his fleeing soul left to appreciate the boundless blue world that is now his, or does the rock that birthed and hardened him blind him to the wonder, and weigh him down to a sham of his earth on the seabed?

Another one drops and hits the sea, and I slide below the waves to watch. He gasps and thrashes the water to a foam, desperate to keep his head in the air. White comet-tails trail from his hands and from his thin stalk legs. I laugh out my dry breath in silver jellyfish bubbles, and take my next as water.

With a beat of my tail I'm beneath him. I wait until he goes under for the third time and sees me. I reach out and smooth the fear from his brow with my fingertips. He smiles, lies becalmed, and I press my lips to his. Eyes wide with wonder he takes my breath, and the cavern of his chest fills with the ocean. I let him go and he falls, slow as a soaked feather, into the depths.

It seems he was the last of them. The ship sails on, stiff timbers slapped by limp ropes, pushed wherever the wind wants. Voiceless.

Far below, in the darkest realms, the heavy glory of the flowing world wraps them in its tight embrace, crushing their bodies to its heart. There is joy in mine knowing that they can now feel what I hear. The low booming songs will burst their bellies, the high clicks and shrieks will pierce the air in their skulls, freeing it in strings of bloody pearls. Bestowing the gift of equilibrium so that they drift with the tides, clothed with waving weed, attended by pecking, glinting fishes and scaled with shells and crabs.

But there is a small voice, insistent. Brimming with salt tears.

I rise to the surface, sweep through the waves, thrust them aside to reach the creaking ship. It leans above me; I place my hand on its wet flanks and look up. A woman stares back, with a girl-child clutched in her arms, who points and squeals, "There! *There!*" The woman shakes her head, disbelief on her face but no fear in her whispered reply.

"That is not your papa."

I beckon, but I have no hold over them. And the knowledge that they have a choice stings my skin with ice. Is this what doubt feels like? How do they bear it?

The woman turns away, puts her child down on their

wooden island and I lose sight of them both. Then, heavy blows reverberate through the hollow body of the ship, followed by the measured rasp of a blade biting over and over – until a roll of thunder rips a shriek from both their throats, and a small boat falls from above, breaching in a clap of spray.

It wallows in silence, lapped by eager waves; the drop must have broken their brittle bodies. I swim to the side, haul myself up to see if they are lying shattered within their white shell.

"He's back mama! Look!"

The woman raises her head, loosens her grip on the child and allows her to scramble to the side where I lean. The boat tips as the girl reaches forward, trying to touch me, and the mother shuffles backwards to balance it. There is pain in her eyes but she does not blink. There is no need for words between us as she feels for the rope lying beside her and throws it to me. I catch it. It's rough and dry against my palms. She nods to me and the girl smiles. "Will you take us to papa?"

I can, but I will not. Their trust is a freshwater sweetness, the taste of estuaries in springtime, of rain that tells of places I will never know; born of jagged inland cliffs higher than the clouds, of liquid songs carried by the wind from seas of stiff leaves that hiss and rush like the oncoming tide.

I twist the rope around my waist and turn away, ready to pull the boat and its riders far from their empty ship, out into my world of endless horizons.

The knife is a bolt of lightning striking my back. Again and again and again.

I cannot cry out - my breath is blood.

I twist. I see her through red water, her arm raised, her blade as bright as a star.

I fall.

She is

so

beautiful.

"Diamonds and Toads, jewels and poisons, kind and unkind girls – sometimes real and imagined boundaries shimmer and blur. Sometimes joy is dark and destructive, sometimes our punishments are beautiful and unfair."

ELODIE OLSON-COONS
Twitter @elllode

Elodie Olson-Coons is a ghostwriter and editor currently based in Switzerland. Her writing has featured in 3:AM Magazine, Music & Literature, The Island Review, [PANK], Paper Darts, and Lighthouse. She is currently working on her first novel, which is about the future, and glacial melt, and borders, and love.

Always Tastes Like Sugar

SHE'S STANDING AT THE SINK, working a raspberry seed from the pit of her molar, when it first happens. Something comes a little loose. A little grit in the mouth, the kind you get from cycling behind a tractor or licking a cut after climbing a fence.

Those boys she likes are on the radio, crying about the taste of a girl's lips. She hums along vaguely, her own lips are a little sore. She doesn't like brass in pop music. She can't handle Christmas carols either though, so the boys stay.

'Dad,' she says, 'come dry for me.'

Lemon meringue, wine in the freezer, the lobsters must still be soughing in their box. Anything else? Her father stroked their backs because he read on the internet that sent them into hibernation. 'It's just,' he said, 'you can hear them breathing.' He had to shoo off the barn cats with a tea-towel.

'How can you listen to this nonsense?' He fiddles with

the radio on the windowsill. She pushes a strand of hair back with a soapy hand. Maybe later they could go for a long stomp in the woods. Maybe that would clear her head. The atmosphere shifts almost physically with each turn of the dial, as if it was the temperature of the room and not the sound that it was changing.

'It's too early for Brahms.'

'You're a horn player', he picks up the towel, 'it's never too early for Brahms.'

'Hornist, please.'

'Don't be ridiculous.'

There's a foot of snow outside. The cats are prowling in it slowly, unsteadily. From the warmth of the kitchen, it is nearly impossible to imagine it being anything but hot, dry powder. Something that might make you cough if you breathed it in.

The girl was a girl amongst other things, in black and gold.

'As long as it doesn't turn seasonal.'

'Brahms is hardly seasonal. What time is your, er, fiancé getting here, anyway?'

'Lunch,' she says quickly, startled. He looks at her. She still can't quite handle Christmas.

'He's got sensible taste in music.'

They were sipping something icy. Surely not dry ice in a cocktail, that burns your stomach lining away. There were little flakes of gold in it.

'I've got sensible taste in music.' She swallows. The back of her throat still tastes a little bitter.

'Are you sure you're alright? You seem a little slow today.' She has a vision of her father sitting on the edge of her bed with a cool washcloth and a bowl of minestrone, stroking her fevered brow. It makes her stomach tight, although she's not sure with what.

'I'm worried about my embouchure. Something about my mouth is... odd.'

It's not untrue. She has a feeling she might have picked up her horn when she stumbled in. How else would her lip be so bruised? Her teeth ache like the aftermath of a bowlful of sugar.

'It's just the wine. The perma-hangover of the season.' He pauses, considers for a while, like a man picking out the less damaged apples from a market stall. 'I didn't hear you come in last night,' he says.

The girl was a girl amongst other things and she seemed to be laced and studded with gold. She had those boots like hooves and her kiss left her upper lip wet and when she licked it was bitter.

She swallows. 'You mean you didn't hear me play taps?' she smiles as hard as she can. Is the oven preheating?

'You laugh,' he says, 'when I was young there was definitely occasional serenading at dawn.'

There was a rhinestone stud between her lower teeth. Is that even possible? It was cold on her tongue.

'Yeah, right. Ride of the stumbling Valkyries, I bet. Spit full of cider dripping from the bell.' On days like these, the mere idea of playing the horn makes her feel sick.

She laughs, turns back to the sink and blinks a few times, as if trying to clear something from her mind – gin, water, fragments of glass. She swallows and swallows but the back of her throat still doesn't taste right. The oven should be preheating.

'Lager. And no.'

'I was joking, Dad.'

Don't mention him again, she pleads. She refuses to think more than two minutes ahead. Her tongue is still gritty. She wonders if this is what it always feels like.

She sets down the last dripping glass bowl and dries her hands. She moves the muscle of her tongue slowly against the roof of her mouth, feeling the grit gather. Her hands tense on the edge of the sink.

'Would you check on the lobsters?' her father says. 'I know it's cowardly, but I can't quite face them again.'

'You'll end up granting them one last tiny cigarette, won't you? I'll do it. Knife 'em in the barn or stick 'em in the freezer?'

'You callous thing,' he says affectionately. 'I knew there was a reason we conceived you.'

'That and someone to pass your horns on to.'

'You make us sound positively Satanic. Now go kill the ... *things* before I really lose my nerve.'

'Maybe it's just pneumonia,' she says.

'Your hangover?'

'The lobsters' breathing.'

'It can't be like drowning,' he muses into his water glass, 'because they were wheezing in and out.'

'We put those wet towels over them,' she says, again. 'We put salt in the tap water. When did I become the cold-hearted one? I'm hungry.'

The way her tongue slipped in made her knees buckle.

'I know, I know. Maybe we can pour some Scotch over them?' he asks hopefully.

'You love lobster,' she reminds him. 'Soft, sweet, taste of the sea. Pools of butter.'

'Oh, I know,' he sighs. 'They will not die for nought.' He wipes his hands on his apron.

'Pour me a glass of Chablis, will you?' she smiles her most golden hostess smile. 'I'll be right back.'

'Dutch courage for the kill? Very well,' he says with a mock-bow.

'In a minute.'

She closes the bathroom door and stands in total pounding silence. She puts her hands to her face, then braces them against the tiles of the wall. She can feel the indents of the pattern of tiny ivy leaves.

What are you trying to be? she whispered against her neck. They were in the bathroom with somebody's rolled-up fifty-pound note, not theirs. Everything was black.

She turns on the light and spits into her hand, quietly. A small piece of grit lies on her soapy palm, oddly shiny.

Be a good girl? Is that what you want?

She waits for her heartbeat to subside. She turns the tap on full and drops the little piece of nothing down the sink. It vanishes.

She just cannot cope with Christmas right now. She needs a glass of water, to go sit in the snow, to put the pie in the oven and check on the lobsters. Everything seems to be milk-scented and lamplit. A flash of a younger self snuggled between her parents on the couch smashes into the back of her mind.

When is he coming?

She mustn't burn the meringues.

She breezes past her father with her best yellow dress and her four-lightbulb smile on. She picks her mother's heavy ceramic dish from the fridge, wobbly with lemon cream and whipped egg. She delicately kicks open the oven and slides it in.

'Chablis for the lady?' He holds out the Sunday wine glass, a little hesitantly.

She feels sort of blinding.

'Actually, I was thinking we could make those icicles.'

She slipped an ice-cold hand up the back of her shirt. It was so cold it hurt. They were laughing like idiots, like children. They were kissing like lovers.

'Icicles?' he blinks.

'Like we did one time. Mum filled glasses with snow and we drank dessert wine out of them.'

Her father's face is inscrutable. 'Maybe that would be nice.' She seems unable to feel her stomach.

She reaches to the top shelves, pulls down the glasses. *She wanted the girl, she wanted the girl.* They're warm and a little bit dusty from the halogens.

She fumbles with the doorknob and nearly falls out into the crisp snow. He stands without moving, still holding the glass of wine.

The air is clear. One of the barn cats stalks by in the distance, stretching its long legs and setting them down as carefully as a tightrope walker. She picks a patch of snow at the foot of a pine tree. Water is already dripping from the boughs, making holes that expose peaks of grass or stone beneath. She tucks her legs under her like a child and starts packing snow into the wine glasses. By childish reflex, she scoops a little snow up in her bare hand and crushes it into the roof of her mouth, where it vanishes instantly, leaving almost nothing.

Would you get me a glass of water? the girl whispered, suddenly slumping. Or something sweet. Lemonade.

She spins the grit around in her tongue. She must have picked up a small pebble, the edges are hard under her tongue. *Lemonade.* She spits, grimacing, into her hand. It's shiny. Birdsong echoes, liquid above her. She wonders what a rhinestone is, and why she didn't think of it as a diamond. She stands unsteadily and stumbles on a little while, towards the forest.

Mother used to pull her up this hill in the red plastic sled with the hole cracked in the corner. They used to leave iced cinnamon crescents and wine outside the door. *Not Christmas*, she pleads.

'Rhinestones, gallstones, icebergs,' she sing-songs, following the thought into darkness, beyond the last visible stalactite. Her tongue traces the grooves of her mouth, searching for more. How can there be more?

Spit pools under her tongue, clean and syrupy. Slowly, she feels another piece growing, with the sickening realisation that it is coming from within her. The edges are sharp. She presses it against her lip.

A memory of the girl's hands between her legs as they pressed up against the speaker's bursts like a geyser inside her.

She is secreting rock. The growth of hysterical laughter makes her stomach buckle. How many times has she climbed these trees?

She spits. Winking like a piece of glass, something falls into the snow and is lost.

'Jewels,' she tries to say, but her tongue is almost fully covered in a thick sheen of new growth. She has to roll it around until it clings together like a pearl and can be spat out. It hurts. She spits and spits, and her hands fill with fragments of clear, shining rock.

Be a good girl. Is that what you want?

In the distance, a car door slams. Something in her gut whirls like a compass then collapses, softening every muscle of her deep into the snow. It stings against her face the way it stung in her throat, and then she can't feel it any more. She stares blurrily into the pile of tiny fragments, not so different from magnified snowflakes themselves.

'Dad will worry,' she thinks. 'Just like rhinestones.' She hums Brahms; imagines her father gingerly hovering the point of the knife above the lobsters.

Something stumbles within her. 'It's OK,' she says.

There's another tiny piece of grit in her mouth. *Be a good girl.* She doesn't even spit.

'Are you OK, honey?' A hand grips her by the shoulder, rolls her face out of the snow. Crouching above her in a grey sweatshirt and jeans, peering down in concern, is the man she loves. She blinks, spits again. 'Your dad said you were outside,' the voice above says hesitantly.

She sits up, braces her back against the tree. 'I got dizzy,' she says vaguely.

'Maybe you need some sugar.'

'I'm going to burn the meringues.'

Methodically, she strips the wet snowflakes from her fingers. The last ones have already melted.

'I just followed your footsteps,' he says somewhat helplessly.

'I'm tired,' she says.

She holds in a mouthful of diamonds and watches how he is silhouetted against the white sky. She needs a glass of wine.

'Darling, what's wrong?'

For one searing moment, she imagines pressing the grit into his mouth, the softness of his shoulder. Pulling him under the covers, giggling back down the stairs. Staring at him blankly as he cracks open his lobster.

'What happened?'

Slowly, unsteadily, she stands. 'Nothing,' she says quietly. She slips her hand into his and swallows.

"I wanted to write a story about a comical, imaginative girl who gets into scrapes."

LENA NG

Lena Ng is from Toronto, Ontario. She has short stories in over two dozen publications including Amazing Stories. "Under an Autumn Moon" is her short story collection. She is currently seeking a publisher for her novel, Darkness Beckons, a Gothic romance.

Tilly and the Frog

TILLY HAD BEEN BANISHED to the garden. The newly-trimmed grass smelled fresh and sharp. The roses, the most conceited of all flowers, bloomed languidly and the sun glowed warm on her skin. In the corner, on top of the tulip tree, a bluebird sang. Tall, neatly trimmed hedges defined the borders of the yard.

Tilly frowned and stomped her feet. She had been naughty at lunch time, slinking underfoot, picking at her peas, speaking with her mouth so full of food that everyone at the table — Mother, Father, and certainly Granny — was astonished by her sheer brattiness.

On her good days, Tilly was a joy to behold, a true blessing of a child. She held doors open for Granny. She picked apples to put on her school teacher's desk, sometimes unbitten. She had cherub, red checks and fat, sausage curls which gave all who met her the impression of a lovely, well-mannered child.

Today, sadly, was not one of those days. In fact, it was a bad day, a terrible day, a contrary day, whereby if the sky was black, she would wish it to be blue or if the sky was blue, she would want it to be purple.

This day had started out in rain when Tilly wanted it to be sun. The house, usually so open and airy, had shrunk in size since everyone was trapped within. Ordinarily so full of excitement and enthralling adventures, her books sat, unopened and unloved on her bedroom floor. Mother was sewing and Father was reading and Granny was sitting, quite possibly thinking. None were a good companion to a six-year-old child.

"What has gotten into you?" asked Father, before her banishment, interrupting his reading and rustling his paper in annoyance after catching Tilly running past him for the fourth time. "Can't you settle down? Go upstairs to your room."

Tilly crossed her eyes, sucked in her nostrils, and made a frightfully rude, unladylike face. Father started out of his chair, suppressing the quirks that appeared at the corners of his mouth. Tilly giggled and raced up the stairs, her elephantine stomps causing Granny to shake her head.

Tilly's room was a little girl's dream, and a little boy's nightmare. On the walls, shell pink, striped wallpaper arose above blush-painted wainscoting. Floor length regal curtains fell from heavy, wooden curtain rods. In the centre of the room, stood a white, four poster bed, draped with luxurious silver-threaded fabric. In the corner of the room, atop a small table with four child-sized chairs graced a tea set made of porcelain, patterned with twisting vines.

A bountiful blessing of books, their bindings lined from many enraptured return visits, filled two bookcases when they were not scattered about on the floor. Tilly invented a few new games to play indoors. She had her tea time with Tabby, where she tied a bonnet over the ungrateful cat's head and tried to coax it to sit at her small table. The game ended abruptly when Tabby hid under the bed.

"Stop bothering the cat," Father said, sticking his head in as he came to check up on her. Tabby's paw took several healthy swipes at Tilly as she leaned under to look at him.

"Bad kitty," she said. "Stay under the bed and think about what you've done."

Next she played dress-up — St. Georgina and the dragon. Mother's tunic, silver and hanging down to Tilly's knees, transformed into a suit of armour. A leftover roll of Christmas wrap served as a sword. Tabby turned into a monstrous, fire-breathing salamander, destroying villages, eating poor children, and giving grannies conniptions. St. Georgina trapped it in a cave under her bed and was preparing to dispatch it.

"Didn't I tell you to leave that poor cat alone?" Father bellowed, turning into a dragon as well. On human days, he was a kind and warm man with lovely laugh lines in the corners of his eyes and mouth, who wore disobedient spectacles which were always attempting to escape off the end of his nose. He read aloud to her tales of fairies and wizards and dragons and never those boring, fine-print articles in the business section of The Times he poured over while eating his toast. On dragon days, he breathed fire and blocked her from all of her fun. "No, Tilly, put that down, it's not an aeroplane." "Tilly, get back here, don't make me chase after you." And now he said, "No, Tilly, the cat is not a dragon." Tabby licked his fur in agreement.

Tilly pouted on the corner of her bed. For now, the dragons had triumphed. Soon the rain passed and the sun uncovered its smiling face but it was too late. Tilly's terrible mood remained.

"Outside," commanded Mother, after the disastrous lunch. "Stay out of the way until I've done the washing up." I will return to vanquish all these dragons, thought St. Georgina.

Granny shook her head when she heard Tilly slam the door. "What's the matter with that child? Some days she's better than butter. Other days she's worse than earwigs. This morning I caught her cracking walnuts with my dentures."

So Tilly was exiled outside to spend her punishment, although being allowed to play outdoors would have been a reward on any other day. The nature of punishments are such that they are contrary to your current inclinations, though they could be rewards when in alignment with them.

"Humph," said Tilly, arms crossed and mouth in a frown. She jumped off the step and kicked at the Queen Anne rosebush.

"Stop kicking at the rosebush," Mother called out from

the kitchen. "I can see what you are up to."

Tilly turned her back away and moved out of sight of the window. Spitefully, she grabbed a handful of the roses and pulled. "Ouch!" she cried, as the thorns scratched her. She stuck her wounded hand in her mouth. Then she turned toward the house and stuck out her tongue.

"And don't wander out of the yard. Play where I can see you."

Of course, the mere mention of forbidding something, to quite-contrary Tilly, ensured the exact opposite. She tiptoed to the great, iron gate and reached up to unlock it. The latch was set too high, however, likely designed to keep little girls captive within. Next, she crept around the perimeter of the hedge, looking for an opening. Behind the tulip tree, a ribbon of light peeked through a gap between the hedges, like a stretched seam on an ample bottom's trousers.

Tilly squeezed her body sideways and, after much fidgeting and squirming, out she popped on the other side. She stood at the top of a gentle hill, the lush green slope descending before her. At the base of the hill, a small grove of trees sprouted. A cheerful brook leading into the grove beckoned her to follow.

Tilly ran down the hill, racing the brook into the woods. She turned somersaults and cartwheels and landed in a heap. Winded, Tilly sat on the bank of the brook at the threshold of the forest. She breathed deeply, waiting for her heart to calm. The trees rustled tenderly, brushed by the breeze, sunlight dappling between its branches to the forest floor. A charming finch sang lilting melodies, sonnets to the leaves.

Plonk. The charming finch flew off at the noise. Plonk, plonk, plonk. Tilly was throwing rocks into the brook.

"Hey! What d'ya think you're doin'?" exclaimed a voice. Tilly looked all around her. She looked left. She looked right. She even looked upon where she was sitting (though I'd think if the voice originated there, it would have said, "Get off.") Finally, she looked at the brook. At the edge, where the water cradled the rocks, sat a great, green, speckled frog, disturbed by the ripples.

Tilly stared at it in disbelief. "A frog? Talking? How are you talking?"

"How are you talking?" the frog answered, rudely. "Haven't you heard any stories about talking frogs?"

"Oh, I remember," said Tilly, recalling a story Father had once read to her. She had fallen asleep well before the ending. "The story of the princess and the frog. It was about a princess who kissed a frog who turned into a handsome prince. Something else happened, I forgot what, then they lived happily ever after. Is that the story you are talking about?" A thought occurred to her and her eyes brightened. "Are you that frog?"

"Ummm... yes," said the frog, a crafty note entering his voice. "The very one indeed. Unfortunately, the witch returned and cast a curse upon me and changed me back into a frog. I'm awaiting a beautiful princess to appear who is brave enough to kiss me and transform me into princely form. But where could I find such a beautiful princess? You wouldn't know any, would you?" He glanced sideways at Tilly.

"I am not a princess but... do you think if I kissed you, you'd turn back into a prince?" said Tilly, looking at the frog with sceptical, yet hopeful eyes.

"Well, it'll have to be a big kiss," replied the frog with an expression that looked as though if he had eyebrows, they would be raised. "A very big kiss." He waggled where his eyebrows would have been, had he any. "Then you must close your eyes and count to three."

Tilly thought for a minute. She didn't want to kiss that great, big, lump of a frog. But the thought of marrying a handsome prince and turning into a princess was tempting. Then she could wave her sceptre about and talk with her mouth full at the dinner table, either separately or together if she were so inclined, without anyone admonishing her.

Tilly pursed her lips into that of a kissing fish. The frog goggled his eyes. She leaned over him and a planted a large, juicy, smack of a kiss right on the tip of his nose. She closed her eyes and counted.

One.

Two.

Three.

The sound of the brook was hushed, as if it was holding

its breath for the magic to work. Tilly opened her eyes.

"Ta da," the frog said, with a low, deep bow. "Thank you, kind lady, for your act of heroism and generosity."

"But nothing happened," said Tilly, somewhat underwhelmed. "You're still a frog."

"What?" said the frog, hopping about in a circle and looking upon himself in astonishment. "You're right. Wait, I know what went wrong. You stay here and I'll be right back." He hopped off.

Tilly looked at the brook. She listened to its burbles, it sounded as if it were chuckling, quietly though, as not to offend her.

Soon, the frog returned. On top of his head sat a sad felt top hat, a bit squashed from poor storage and lack of proper care. "That's better. What is a prince without a crown?" he said. He took off the hat and bowed again, deeply. "Thank you, dear lady, for rescuing me from my horrible life as a common frog. The rooms, so damp and draughty. And the food, terrible. The flies are definitely not USDA prime." A buzzing noise distracted him. His eyes followed the sound. His long, red tongue shot out and snatched an unlucky bug, a cicada who had the poor timing of choosing that moment to emerge from its seventeen-year-long sleep.

"Maniemay," the frog continued, "mow yat fings r diffewent..."

"I can't understand you," Tilly said, frowning, not enjoying the view of chewed up insect. She was beginning to see the point of not speaking with one's mouth full.

The frog swallowed. "I said, now that things are different, it will only be quality bugs for me. No more of that marked-down, last-day-of-sale business. No more worms or grubs or crawling nasties for me. Only plump, ripe butterflies who dine on nectar and fruit—"

"Are you sure you are a prince?" interrupted Tilly. "You still look like a frog to me."

"Of course I am. I thought you read the story? It's called The Frog Prince." The frog spoke slowly to demonstrate his point. "The Frog," he pointed to himself, "Prince." He pointed to his hat.

"But... aren't you supposed to turn into a man?"

"A man? Eeeew," asked the frog, shivering at the thought. "Why would I turn into a man? Do men turn into frogs when they become princes? No, I become frog royalty. I think you've got the story wrong."

"But aren't we supposed to get married? Isn't that what happens next?" Tilly asked, the appeal of becoming a princess still outweighing the thought of having a short, clammy husband.

"What? What are you talking about? Of course not," said the frog, genuinely horrified. "The missus wouldn't stand for that. No, the princess kisses the frog who turns into a frog prince who goes home to his wife who is impressed by his crown and listens to him for a change instead of telling him to bring home something other than flies for supper." He

255

raised his right arm and pointed to the sky in a pompously commanding gesture. "'We will have flies when I want to have flies,' I will say to her—"

"I don't think that was in the book," said Tilly, with a furrowed brow, having stayed awake through enough fairy tales to know there was always a marriage before the happy ending. "I will have to have Father read it to me again."

"You do that. I must be going," the frog said. "The missus doesn't like it when I'm away too long. She'll say I've been out kissing the ladies."

"She would be right. You have been."

"I certainly have not," the frog replied, chest puffed out in indignation. "They have been kissing me. Good day." He then jumped into the brook with a giant splash and swam the frog stroke home.

"For my Dad, who taught me that women were strong, words powerful, and the art of storytelling precious."

G.K. SIHAT
www.gksihat.com

A Londoner to the core, G.K. Sihat has always been madly in love with the written word. When she's not writing, reading or daydreaming, you can find her mesmerised by an artistic masterpiece, curled up with a boxset or walking through the rain with her headphones in.

The Angel and the Teller of Tales

NOT ONCE HAD HE TOUCHED HER, yet Rawiya felt the ghostly grip on her upper arm tighten. She was compelled forwards, blindly following the guard that had taken her from her home.

The room they finally stopped inside was warmer than the ones they paused in earlier. Scents that reminded her of a past life, now a distant memory, wafted through the air, dancing up her nose. The atmosphere changed as her guard slipped behind her, and the darkness she'd become rather accustomed to was torn away.

Rawiya blinked, her eyes tearing up a little more with each flutter of her eyelashes. It had been over a week since they forced the blindfold over her eyes, over a week since she made the choice that landed her here – in the devil's lair.

It took a few moments before her eyes adjusted. Colour came back first – reds and golds with chocolate brown trimmings, and then more significant details – the high ceilings, the door-less entrances, the extravagant furnishings. Lastly, the smaller things – the beading on the sofa cushions, the carvings on the coffee table, the statues of the women on the fireplace, each one in a different Kathak pose. Whatever Rawiya expected, this was not it.

Only when her guard motioned for her to join them did Rawiya notice the seven girls standing in a semi-circle in the centre of the room. No two were similar – not in age or ethnicity, nor build or hair colour. Not even their clothing bore any likeness. The only thing they shared in common was the guard standing two feet behind them – head bowed, hands clasped behind his or her back. Rawiya moved to take her place at the end, the invisible bonds shackling her to her guard falling free as he joined his comrades.

A woman appeared, raven coloured hair tumbling over a mask of pure white that covered the left-hand side of her face from hairline to blood red lip. Her lean figure was outfitted in form-fitting leather, every inch of visible skin covered in tattoos – a script Rawiya struggled to tear her eyes from. On first glance, it appeared to be some form of Arabic – it's cursive style more like a painting than words. But soon, Rawiya realised the letters did not run from right to left, but downwards.

"You are here to serve," she said, examining each of them in turn. "You are here to entertain." She walked down the line, holding their gazes until it became uncomfortable. "Until you have been called to our Lord, you will remain here." She stepped backwards so they could each see her. "You will live in luxury because it pleases our Lord, but as soon as it stops pleasing him, you will leave." Rawiya felt the girl beside her tense. "In the meantime, you will have whatever you wish – expensive jewels, fine wines, extravagant dress – all you have to do is ask." Rawiya watched her lip curl as if she were trying to fake a smile to hide a sick joke. "Here, you are queens among men."

Rawiya followed her silhouette as she made for the door. The shadow of a whip trailed behind her like a tail. Yet, a whip, Rawiya noticed as the guards followed her out the door, was nowhere to be seen. The echo of the door slamming reverberated through her bones.

So, it began.

* * *

Three weeks passed before the first girl was called.

Shauna – a pale girl from the West with blonde hair, blue eyes, and sharp nails. She was loud and opinionated, with the ability to steer every conversation towards herself. Within three days, they knew everything about her. From the reason she left her boyfriend broken-hearted and her love of singing, to how she called the manager of some poor cashier trying to explain they received their stock late and wouldn't have leggings in her size until next month.

Still, when she was called, the girls waited anxiously around the coffee table for her to return, retiring to their rooms only when night began to turn into morning. When they woke hours later, they flocked to her bedroom only to find it still empty.

Shauna never returned – but that hadn't stopped Gabriella from being summoned.

She was the most voluptuous woman Rawiya had ever seen. Her curves accentuated by the long black locks that fell in waves over one shoulder and the cropped tops and tiny shorts that showed off her tanned skin. Having never used anything other than kohl, Rawiya asked the beauty for a make-up lesson. Gabriella replied that she was already a *knock-out*, though she still obliged.

But Gabriella hadn't returned either, and now the third night crept upon them, fear filling the eyes of every girl left behind.

"He's killing us, isn't he?"

Emiko's question resounded through the room. At nineteen, she was the youngest of the group. She reminded Rawiya of one of her sister's dolls, long and thin with unnaturally straight hair that fell to the curve of her back. Her amber eyes were big and beautiful, her cheeks coated in a natural red sheen. There was such innocence in her that Rawiya longed to know how she had come to be among the eight.

She had no hope of answering Emiko's question. Instead, she slipped her fingers through the girl's and squeezed gently. "I won't let anything happen to you."

Emiko gave her a small smile as they joined the four remaining girls for tea and savoury snacks Rawiya could not name. All waited with bated breath, aware their name could be called any second. Swallowing became harder with each bite. When the last girl finished her final piece, the doors flung open and the masked woman appeared, flanked by two guards.

As she had done the previous times, she looked the girls over one at a time, sifting through her options. As soon as her gaze returned to Emiko, Rawiya's ears filled with silent screams.

"Her."

The guards took a single step forward, invisible bonds obviously snapping into place around Emiko. She rose from her seat, though she seemed to be struggling as she did so. The fear in her face rooted the other girls to their spots, but it shot Rawiya to her feet.

"Take me!" Rawiya regretted the words even as she spoke them again. "Take me."

A sharp eyebrow raised on the woman's face, her hand following to halt the guards. "You want to meet our Lord?"

"I'm ready."

A cruel smile appeared on her face. "They all say that... but they soon learn."

* * *

Rawiya swallowed her laugh as she followed her captors through one dimly-lit passageway after another. She knew the answer now. Her lack of blindfold confirmed it. There was only one reason she could think of that would explain why they wouldn't hide the route to their leader – she was marching to her death.

Succumbing to the power of the bonds, Rawiya closed her eyes. Twice she had stepped between the Reaper and his victim. Twice she had to face the unknown – the consequences of her choices. She prayed for the safety of her sister and Emiko, sweet and innocent as they both were, for a painless end, and for God to answer 'yes' to her prayers, instead of the 'no' she was so often given.

When Rawiya opened her eyes again, double doors made of dark wood towered above her. The guards pushed them aside as if they were nothing more than paper. A hallway sat, uninviting, on the other side. With piqued curiosity, Rawiya stepped through them without encouragement, her bonds falling free as she crossed the threshold.

For a fraction of a second, she debated running. She imagined herself returning home, Emiko by her side. She imagined starting a new life somewhere safe. Somewhere they could not follow. But that was a fantasy – something that could never be. Rawiya had made her choice, and there was no turning back. As if reiterating her thoughts, the doors slammed shut behind her.

She was growing accustomed to the darkness now.

Sounds and smells all somehow felt familiar within it – comforting. Flickering light came from the right and she moved towards it, discarding her fear on the floor behind her. If this were to be her end, she would face it with courage.

Bare wall blended into yet more bare wall; hard floor made way for yet more hard floor. If it hadn't been for the suddenly high ceiling, the fire roaring on mute in the fireplace, and the rug partially covering the floor, it wouldn't have been easy to distinguish the hallway from the room it opened up into. It was empty, save for two throne-like chairs and the low table between them. Rawiya could just about make out a bowl of fruit in the centre of it and a glass on either side. She edged closer, realising all too suddenly that he was already there, lounging in the chair furthest away.

His dark hair sat in shoulder-length waves, a few strands tumbling over his lowered face. Dark shadows cut across his face, emphasising his sharp cheekbones, strong jaw, and long nose. He rose to his feet and when he looked at her, Rawiya fought the urge to lower her gaze. Instead, she focused on the wall behind him, noticing the strange shadows that lurked there. His form was undeniable – perfectly proportioned but with two strange shapes protruding from where his shoulder blades were.

Wings.

Rawiya's breath caught. Her mother had told her a story once about angels cast out of Heaven, cursed to live amongst the humans they hated so much. But stories, powerful as she believed them to be, were just that – stories. Sentences shaped to entertain and educate – and often, far-fetched. Tales of dragons living in the highest mountain ranges; swords gifted to boy kings from a lady that lived in a lake; sea serpents so large, they could circle the earth and grasp their tails in their mouths.

As he circled her, Rawiya forced herself to focus on her captor. On the man who would bring Death to her. He was every bit the mythical King. His black shirt open, revealing the toned, bare chest beneath, his skin tanned. Trousers hung low on his hips, leading to bare feet.

No wings.

He lifted a hand, and Rawiya took an involuntary step away. One side of his lips lifted into the ghost of a smirk as his long fingers pushed his hair back from his eyes. Before she could see them clearly, it fell right back. But it was when he cocked his head to the side that Rawiya knew he was toying with her. Eventually, he returned to his seat, grabbing an orange from the bowl as he threw his leg over the arm of the chair.

"So, you're the volunteer," he said, peeling back the orange's skin and placing a segment of the fruit into his mouth. "Tell me, what's your talent?"

Rawiya's eyebrow raised on its own volition, and she silently cursed it as his smile grew a little wider. "Talent?"

"Your predecessor was a skilled belly dancer," he told

her. "The one before sang ... to say she was mediocre would be being generous."

"Are they dead?"

The words left Rawiya's mouth before she thought them through. The smirk on her captor's face disappeared, the wing-shaped shadows on the wall twitching. Not once did he look at her.

"Death is considered a welcome release for many."

Rawiya shuddered under the pressure of the words. "I have no talent," she replied, "my life held little room for fanciful hobbies."

"Come, everyone has a talent." She felt his gaze fall on her. "You have a sister, yes?" Another shudder. "How did you calm her when she woke from a nightmare? How did you entertain her when her make-believe friends turned their backs on her? How did you keep her mind occupied when her world was falling apart?"

The answer to his questions touched a nerve. She had continued to do as her mother had done. She had stroked her hair with one hand while tracing invisible infinity signs on the inside of her wrist. She...

"...told her stories."

* * *

Once upon a time, an accountant and his wife welcomed a baby boy into the world. The boy was generous and loving, touched by God in ways they could scarcely believe. As he grew, he became a Teacher, travelling far and wide, spreading love and understanding, charity and wisdom, and, above all, faith.

One day, weary from his travels, the Teacher chose to settle in a small village for a night. There, he received two invitations for lunch - one from a poor carpenter, the other from a rich landlord. He had never differentiated between rich and poor, nor between the castes religion separated them into. So, he accepted both invitations and asked the carpenter to join him at the landlord's home.

The landlord organised a grand feast, his table piled high. As the Teacher sat down, the carpenter arrived, two single pieces of flatbread in his hands. He offered them to the Teacher, who began to eat.

Confused and angry, the landlord confronted him. 'I have served you such rich foods and yet you eat flatbread from a poor man's hand!'

Without a word, the Teacher took the carpenter's remaining flatbread in one hand and picked one from the landlord's plate with the other. He raised them in front of him and squeezed. Shock flooded through the room as milk flowed from the carpenter's food, and blood poured from the landlord's.

'You exploit the labourers who work for you,' the Teacher told the landlord. 'You beat them, withhold food as punishment, dock their wages when you are displeased

with them. It is their blood that flows here. But the carpenter is the labourer. He works hard for his money, provides for his family, puts his blood, sweat, and tears into everything he does. Therefore milk flows from his.' The Teacher placed the flatbreads down and stood. *'True wealth lies in serving those less fortunate than yourself. If you stop suppressing others and begin to help them, you will always remain happy and prosperous...'*

Rawiya dared to look away from the flames, glancing at her captor. His face remained expressionless. It wasn't the neatest telling of a tale. She never had reason to perfect her endings; her sister had always fallen asleep long before she had gotten that far, but she had hoped it was enough to satisfy him – enough for him to spare her.

"Do you remember the way back to your room?"

Unable to find the words, Rawiya replaced her missing speech with a nod. He stood, stepping so deep into the darkness she didn't realise he was still there until he spoke. "Until tomorrow then."

* * *

When Rawiya walked back into the chambers the girls shared, no one was waiting for her. No one expected her to return. She hadn't been expecting it. Nor had the guards posted outside, who exchanged confused looks before one of them let her into the room and the other raced down the hall, no doubt making sure she hadn't harmed their leader.

Rawiya made straight for Emiko's chamber. The girl's sleeping figure, so small in the king-sized bed, was curled in a ball as if it would somehow protect her from the cruelties of the world, of the fate she so narrowly escaped that evening. Rawiya felt the fear she had reclaimed as she returned through the hallway creeping up on her. She fell asleep in the chaise lounge that sat at the foot of Emiko's bed, the pillows soft and inviting.

* * *

"Did he say anything about Shauna and Gabriella?"

"He only said they had entertained him."

She would spare the other girls his comment about death being a welcome release. The hope that they, too, would somehow survive was the only hope she could offer them now. Hearing her reply, the girls returned to their meals, no more questions voiced.

Her bonds were tighter that night, and Rawiya couldn't help but wonder if it was some form of punishment for being allowed to live. The double doors flung open, and Rawiya caught the annoyance on the masked woman's face as she stepped through them.

Comfortable armchairs had replaced the throne-like seats of the previous evening, a longer table between them housed two full plates of food flanked by two candelabras. Her captor sat on what she now understood to be his 'usual side'; his shirt, the colour of dried blood, buttoned halfway.

"Join me."

Taking a deep breath, Rawiya did as she was bid – even taking a bite of the delicacies piled high on her plate when he motioned towards it. Every morsel of food she had eaten since being taken by the Fallen had been other-worldly, but this was something else entirely. Her mouth watered a little more with each bite and her heart beat with excitement as her stomach warmed with pleasure.

"Curious creature," she thought she heard her captor mumble as she finished the food on her plate. He sat back on his seat, swirling his wine around its glass. "Have you a new story for me tonight?"

Rawiya took a sip of her wine, the story dripping into her mind, taking its time to form fully. It had been one her mother told her often – a childhood favourite.

* * *

Once upon a time, there lived two brothers. The elder was a strong warrior, commander-in-chief of one of the most prestigious armies in the East. The younger was kind and creative. Wise beyond his years. But despite their differences, they were loved equally by their parents.

One day, a man gifted the family an apple. 'Whosoever

eats the apple will harness the power of supreme knowledge and immortality,' he explained.

Both brothers were desperate to claim the reward. An argument erupted between them. To pacify the situation, their father made them a deal – whoever could circle the world three times and returned first would be given the fruit.

Without wasting a second, the elder brother began his journey. The younger, though, did not move. He knew there was no beating his brother physically, but he could do so with intelligence – and so, he circled his parents.

'What are you doing?' his father asked him.

The younger son simply smiled and finished his third circle. When he stood before them again, he finally spoke. 'When you ask a child what the centre of their universe is, they reply their mother,' he told them. 'For me, it is the two of you. With you is my entire universe, so not only have I circled the world thrice, I have circled the universe.'

Pride filled his parents, but his brother was furious when he returned. He argued that he had been cheated out of what was rightfully his, but his parents disagreed. Knowing how deeply he meant his words; they gifted their youngest the fruit...

"That story means something to you."

A smile kissed Rawiya's lips. "It was one of my mother's favourites," she told him. "Every night she would tell me a new story. Tales about gods and monsters, dragons and mermaids, noble princes and beautiful princesses."

"That's a lot of stories."

There was no emotion in his voice. No sarcasm, no teasing. Rawiya accidentally caught his eye. They were so dark – almost black. An unnatural fire blazed within them.

"A thousand of them, my father once told me."

"Why did she stop?"

Rawiya's stomach lurched. "You can't tell stories when your own has ended."

An emotion Rawiya couldn't quite decipher flashed across her captor's face, disappearing as quickly as it had appeared. He stood, moving towards the darkness.

"You may go."

"What's your name?"

Though he stopped, he remained silent. Seconds turned to minutes. Just when Rawiya thought he would refuse to answer, he spoke, his voice gentler than she could have ever imagined.

"Arius."

He was gone before the echo died.

* * *

The following day came and went with little consequence. The girls had begun to avoid Rawiya at all costs. Emiko tried to tell her she imagined it, but Rawiya knew better. They

273

no longer looked at her, even when speaking to her. They developed sudden memory loss, remembering they needed to do something important when she joined them; each and every one of them, Emiko included, fell silent when she entered the room. So Rawiya spent the days alone until it was time to return to Arius.

Flowers sat in a crystal vase at the edge of the table today – tall green stalks, the upper quarter covered in a line of red and yellow. Only four of five on each stalk had flowered, fiery scarlet in colour. Rawiya reached out a finger to stroke one of the long-bladed leaves that sprouted from the base – so tall that had they not bowed over, they would have covered the flowers completely.

"Crocosmia Lucifer."

Involuntarily, Rawiya sucked in a breath. She stood, catching her captor's gaze once again. There was something akin to amusement in it today. He approached her, his movements slow and deliberate. Rawiya gulped. She had never felt so much like prey before. Arius tilted his head, his eyes not leaving hers as he spoke.

"They can grow up to four feet tall in soil, with a spread a little over half that amount. And the flowers are known to attract the rarest of hummingbirds and butterflies."

"They're beautiful."

"They're yours."

Rawiya's mouth fell open, looking from the flowers to Arius and back again. He was so close she could smell him.

As she recognised the scents of samphire and water mint, Arius sat down, a heavy sigh following his exhale.

"Dinner will be late this evening."

"Has something happened?"

Arius snorted. "You'd care if something had?"

Rawiya took her usual seat, taking the time to mull over her answer. Eventually, she nodded. "I would."

"Worried how it would impact yourself and your friends?"

"And you."

Arius' head snapped back, his brows creasing together. "I took you prisoner. I killed your friends. And you'd worry how a problem affected *me?*"

She knew how ridiculous it sounded. Her father would tell her that it was nothing. A minor case of Stockholm Syndrome at best. But she knew better – he was just as trapped as they were.

Once upon a time, a prince, who had long since relinquished his riches and comforts, sat beneath a Bodhi tree. There he meditated; his mind clear of everything. Seven daughters of sin came to tempt him away from his peace, but he did not see them. He did not hear their sweet songs. Nor did he smell their rose and jasmine skin, or the ash they turned into when they failed their task.

Soon afterwards, he was visited by the army of death, their arrows nocked and aimed for his heart, his head, and his stomach. They blocked out the sun as they flew through the air, breaking into a million lotus blossoms cascading from the skies and blanketing the ground. The army fell, defeated. But as the moon rose, it brought with it a final guest –

Three thunderous booms interrupted Rawiya's tale. Her heart raced. It's sound so loud, she almost mistook the knocking as the beating of it echoing in her ears. She missed the sound of the doors flying open and boots hitting the floor until a man spoke from behind her.

"Forgive me, my lord."

"What is it?" Arius asked, his gaze shifting from Rawiya.

"The commander is here."

Veins rose in the backs of Arius' hands, running along his muscular forearms. Rawiya took in the tightness in his jaw and the thin shape his lips pulled into. He didn't say a word as he stormed out of the room.

* * *

No orders had been given for her to leave. No orders had been given for her to stay either.

It was likely that the 'return to your room' instruction had been implied when Arius had stormed out, but it made no difference. Rawiya did not return to her bedroom that night. She waited until the candles burnt through their last inch of wick and the flames died in their hearth. She waited until the Crocosmia flowers faded into darkness, and then she waited some more. Sleep claimed her as she pulled her legs up to her chest and held onto them, her fear of the darkness poking at her as it always had.

Chirping birds woke her the following morning. At first, Rawiya thought she was dreaming – it was impossible for a windowless room to host such sounds – but as she turned over on her back and silk stroked her skin, she realised she was no longer in the armchair she had fallen asleep in. The smells floated off them – samphire and water mint.

Rawiya sat up, her eyes darting around the room. The bedroom she found herself in was simply designed, yet somehow even grander than the ones the girls had been given. Black curtains were pulled over the floor-to-ceiling windows, the sun slipping through the gaps between them. A tan leather chair, reading lamp, and small table covered in books sat in the farthest corner, but other than the bed and its side table, bare of everything but a glass of water, that was all. A luxurious rug greeted her bare feet as Rawiya slipped out from beneath the black sheets, her breath catching as she realised her extravagant dress had been swapped out for a black tunic.

With a deep breath, she parted the veil that separated the bedroom from an otherwise open area – a kitchen, living space, and bar, all currently unoccupied with the same black and tan furnishings. Three doors stood side-by-side on the other end of the room. One, she assumed, would lead to the bathroom. Another was the way out. As she debated what the third door would lead to, it opened.

Arius stepped out, dressed in the same manner he had been the first time they met, though his hair looked as though he had been pulling at it. He froze when he saw Rawiya.

"You're awake."

The wall of books through the door behind him caught Rawiya's eye. Arius followed her gaze. "I used to collect first editions," he told her.

"Used to?"

He closed the door behind him, moving swiftly into the kitchen area. "I don't have anything to eat, but I have coffee..." Rawiya's gaze darted down to the tunic she wore, which suddenly felt short despite falling below her knee. "I had Atiena change you," he said quickly. "I hear corsets are a nightmare to sleep in."

Atiena. The masked woman. Despite everything, Rawiya snorted a laugh at the thought of her unlacing her corset. Arius relaxed, and she followed his lead. He had done nothing to harm her. The girls had been taken on his orders, perhaps, but still, she trusted him.

Pouring coffee into two cups, Arius spoke. "Will you tell me the rest of your story?"

* * *

As the moon rose, it brought a final guest with it.

A pool of water formed in front of the prince; the surface so steady it resembled a mirror. The prince lowered his fingers to it, and his reflection reached back until their fingers interlocked. With a knowing smile, the prince pulled.

'Will you not show me your true face?' he asked when his reflection sat before him.

'This is my true face,' the reflection replied. 'I am the temple. You live within me.'

The prince smiled, true and genuine. 'Oh, Lord of my own ego. You are but an illusion. A representation of the darkness that sits within this temple made of our flesh and blood and bone. But that does not make you me, nor does it make me you.'

The darkness shrunk in size. Hair grew thick on his chin, his head, and his chest. His skin darkened, his eyes following seconds later.

'You cannot live without me,' he spat.

'No,' the prince agreed, 'but I can choose not to feed you.'

The darkness shrunk further, his anger rising. 'You will die.'

'As all things do,' the prince replied. 'But death is simply the shedding of this body. The soul will live on. And it is the soul we must nourish –"

Rawiya stopped. Arius stared at her, his eyes welling up with tears. His emotion stuck in his throat, bobbing up and down as he straightened in his chair. "And the reflection... the darkness. What happened to him?"

"He disappeared," Rawiya replied. "Faded into nothingness. The prince acknowledged him for what he was and, in doing so, defeated him."

"And what was he?"

"Part of him. A part we all have that obscures the knowledge of truth. The part that deceives, disguises, and threatens. The part that terrifies us or causes confusion. That uses fear as a weapon, that causes us suffering and pain. That makes us believe that death is –"

"That death is?"

Rawiya smiled. "You told me that death was a welcome release." When Arius didn't reply, she continued. "The end."

"And it's not?"

"It's just another inevitable change," she replied. "A new beginning."

Silence settled over them. The birds, too, fell quiet. It was a long time before Arius broke it. "Tell me your story."

Rawiya thought for a moment, sifting through tale after tale in her mind until she settled on one about the demon king that kidnapped his rival's queen. As soon as the words 'once upon a time,' left her lips, Arius lifted his hand.

"*Your* story."

Shrugging, Rawiya replied, "There's little to tell."

"Tell me anyway."

The words tumbled from Rawiya's lips, her stomach somersaulting with the start of each new sentence. "My mother was an heiress, rich beyond anyone's wildest dreams. She married my father young. He and his family weren't well off, though they didn't struggle either. His brothers, however, were... less than pure. They convinced my mother to invest in their ventures and lost her inheritance.

"My mother took a cleaning job to help my father. He was ashamed, I think... one day, she was cleaning a toilet and went into labour. She lost too much blood to be saved. Her last wish was that my sister would have the childhood they weren't able to give me. My grandmother raised us while my father fought tooth and nail to provide but it wasn't enough, so I offered myself to your men."

"You're lying."

A jolt of fear shot through Rawiya. "I don't know what you mean," she replied, forcing a calm expression onto her face.

"My men told me about you," Arius said, his own breathing steady, his gaze resolute. "They said it was your father who lost your mother's inheritance. That he had a gambling problem which got out of hand. They also told me he took his own life six years ago. That it was *you* who fought tooth and nail to provide for your sister. That it was your grandmother who tried to sell your sister to them, but you volunteered to go to spare her."

The truth always had a way of making its victim weak. Rawiya battled against the nausea. She waged war against the urge to look away – to run away. She held her ground, praying she didn't look as weak as she felt.

"Why would you do such a thing?"

And so she told him, "Love is unconditional."

* * *

Arius didn't call for her that evening. He didn't call for her the evening that followed, either. Or the one after that.

With the girls avoiding her still, Rawiya kept herself confined to her bedroom. Emiko was her only company, joining her for a short while once or twice a day, the look of worry on her face becoming more and more pronounced with each passing visit. But, soon, she stopped. And when the seventh day arrived, and Arius still hadn't called her, Rawiya's fear returned.

She walked from the empty living room to the empty kitchen, calling for her friend. "Emiko?" she called louder, wandering into her friend's bedroom. "Emiko?" Empty. She ran from room to room, not a single one of the girls in them. "Emiko!"

She was alone.

Fear grew larger, producing claws. It scratched at her from the inside, threatening to rip her into pieces.

Rawiya grabbed a candle, running to the room in which

she'd met Arius. Empty. Even the furniture had gone. But she found a door deep in the shadows, the one her captor often slunk into. She reached out, taking a deep breath as she turned the handle and stepped through. She knew where the darkness led now.

Arius' private chambers.

He stood at one of the floor-to-ceiling windows, a glass of deep brown liquid in his hand. Rawiya watched as he brought the glass to his lips, drinking deeply. He seemed lost in his thoughts, and she had come in so quietly – had he even heard her?

"Where are the girls?"

He turned to face her; his face free from any answer to her silent question. "I sent them home. They've been compensated for their time here, and no harm has come to them."

Rawiya searched for the lie in every inch of his face but saw nothing to suggest he was anything other than truthful. "Why?"

Arius set his glass on the coffee table, collapsing into the sofa. "That is a harder question to answer."

"Then I suggest you make more of an effort."

He laughed. It was slow and soft. Innocent, like a child's. When he looked at her, there was no shadow of evil in his gaze, no burning fire. It was simply Arius. The man she now realised she had been growing inexplicably fond of.

"In all the years your mother told you tales of times long

forgotten and lands long since lost to the sea, did she ever tell you one about the angel that fell in love with a mortal?"

One-half of his lips curled into a smile as if memories filled him. "His parents and siblings had warned him what would happen. They told him that mortals could not live in the white and angels could not exist in the grey. But he ignored them. He ignored them because he, too, believed that love was unconditional. And so he chose her. And, in turn, she drained the white from him before running away with another."

Upon seeing the grief etched on his face, Rawiya took a few steps closer.

"He tried to go home, but the doors were forever closed to him. And when neither his parents nor siblings came to his aid, their warnings echoing in his ears, he made a choice."

"What kind of choice?"

"If angels can't exist in the grey and the white is unwelcoming, only one option remains." Arius' face darkened. Though Rawiya knew it was impossible, the entire room seemed to darken with it. "He hunted her down. Slaughtered everyone she loved, then drew the blade across her throat. And when that didn't bring him the satisfaction he craved, he vowed to punish all daughters of Maya. To take the virtue they offered him, then reward them with a quick, painless death."

"Shauna and Gabriella." The names rose like bile in

Rawiya's mouth, but she did not pale when he turned to face her again. "But the other girls are alive."

"They are."

"Then you've broken the pattern," she said to him, her voice low. "You're no longer in the black."

"You should leave."

"What if I don't want to?"

* * *

Despite her words, Rawiya obeyed without waiting for Arius' answer. Still, he played the moment in his head again and again for the hours that followed.

What if I don't want to?

It was foolish of her to choose darkness. It was foolish of him to believe she would. But he was captivated by her tales, by her strength of character, and by her willingness to sacrifice herself so others could survive.

As each of her qualities dripped into his mind, Arius felt his heart stirring. It was different from the last time. He did not feel weak from it. He felt strong. Stronger than he ever had. The kind of woman that caused such a reaction could not be bought by trinkets or gold or jewels. Nor would a simple declaration suffice. But as he stepped out onto the balcony of his bedroom for the first time in years, breathing in the fresh air and basking in the warm sun on his face, Arius knew exactly which gesture would be well received.

He called Atiena to him, the corner of her lip twitched, her fingers tightening on her hip as she heard his request. "Have you not learned your lesson, my Lord?"

"They are doors that are forever closed to me, Atiena," he replied, staring up at the cloudless sky. "But there is hope for a brighter future without them."

"And if she will not have you? If this is all just a ploy to protect the others?"

"Then I have been bested by an equal, and I shall be gracious when I admit defeat."

Nothing more was spoken between them, and when Atiena returned days later with a girl that was both a stranger to him, yet so familiar, Arius found a small bud of hope opening up inside him.

* * *

For the better part of two decades, Rawiya had been swimming in a pool of stories – tales of good and evil, hope and fear – narratives that warned her of the darkness in those who seemed light, while assuring her there was light in those who seemed dark. Not once had she imagined she would be the heroine in one of those stories. Not once did she think she would be standing before a man considered a beast by all, but a prince by her – for she saw the light in him. She had seen it the very first evening they met. It was a light somewhat like that of a child's – fresh, playful, and curious.

Now, as she stood before the dark prince, his right hand nervously clenching and unclenching, Rawiya knew this particular story was coming to an end.

She had known it from the second she saw her sister standing in his chambers – from the disapproving glare Atiena had thrown in her direction before leaving the room, from the loose grip with which her sister held her hand. Whatever had transpired between her and Arius had been enough to make the girl feel at ease. Rawiya glanced over her shoulder, catching the surreptitious wink her sister threw at her. She raised her eyebrows in warning.

"Your grandmother has been well taken care of," Arius said, snapping her attention back to him. "She will want for nothing till the end of her days. And Emiko, who has no family of her own, will be invited to come and stay, if you so wish."

How timid he looked all of a sudden. So unlike himself. Or, perhaps, more so. With one last squeeze, Rawiya let go of her sister's hand and moved towards him. One more step and she would be in his arms. Arius, too, must have grown aware of the lack of space between them. He raised his eyes to meet hers, words tumbling from his mouth in barely a whisper.

"Is it possible for a teller of tales to love one fallen from grace?"

Rawiya knew it was in darkness and despair that light

and hope shone brightest. She knew life was filled with not just black, white, and grey, but every colour imaginable. She knew that 'happily ever after' was a construct made by storytellers to keep that light and colour vibrant long after the tales had come to an end. But she also knew when one story ended, another began, and as she stared into Arius' eyes, her heart lurched, and she felt ready for her next story to begin. For, on the tip of her tongue sat a single word, and she spoke it with a full, unburdened heart.

"Unconditionally."

"I wrote a story about lost souls finding each other in unlikely places. I want readers to know that something sweet can come out of even the sourest situation."

AVRA MARGARITI
Twitter @avramargariti

Avra Margariti is a queer Social Work undergrad from Greece. She enjoys diverse storytelling in all its forms.

Pears and Seafoam

I'VE BEEN IN THE PEAR ORCHARD for three days and two nights when I see her. Her hair is made of gold, her hands made of silver.

She stands by the creek bank, her dainty shoes balanced on the stones among the wild brush and cattails. She presses her palms together, the moonlight glinting off them as surely as it is reflected in the creek. Her eyes are closed, her face set into an expression of intense focus, her pink lips trembling with a stream of words too quiet for me to hear.

She's beautiful.

My nails bite into the bark of the pear tree I hide behind. It rubs my fingertips raw as I watch her pray by the water.

I want to shake her, shout in her face, "Don't you know God doesn't care? His angels aren't listening. Only the sea witches hear you."

God won't give me my eternal soul. He won't return my voice or my tongue. He won't make the prince—or anyone at all, for that matter—love me.

If I were back home in the ocean, my tail would give a powerful snap of frustration. My all-too-human legs twist beneath me, muscle memory playing a cruel joke on me. The undergrowth rustles.

Turning around, she calls, "Is somebody there?"

I scurry deeper into the copse, my heart thumping against my throat, my feet leaving a trail of blood on the long grass.

I fall asleep beneath the dark tangle of branches at the base of the oldest pear tree. Each night, I wake up screaming without a voice, tasting the memory of saltwater. Tonight, I feel the weight of a blanket draped over me and inhale the calming scent of honeysuckle. I jerk upright, the crashing waves and rapid undertow an unrelenting echo in my ears.

"I didn't mean to scare you. I couldn't sleep so I took a walk," the girl from the creek says. She nods toward the blanket. "It's cold tonight."

For the longest time, we regard one another, neither of us moving closer or backing away.

A heavy cloak is pulled tight around her, and spun-gold hair flows over one shoulder. My eyes trace her high forehead, proud nose and soft lips. She's older than me but not by much. Nineteen. Maybe twenty.

"The girls who work in the orchard talk. They say you're a vindictive spirit roaming the grounds."

I wonder if she knows what the workers call her behind her back.

"You don't seem evil," she says. "Just lonely." Her voice

is soft, melodious, weaving itself into the nocturnal song of the insects and the breeze through the trees.

She wouldn't say this if she knew what I was: the naïve fish, lovesick girl, jaundiced monster. She wouldn't be so kind if she saw my empty mouth and soulless chest.

I open and close my mouth like a sea anemone, no sound coming out. I think I taste sea foam. Loosening my jaw again, I let the moonlight illuminate the vacant cavern.

I expect her to gasp, cry out, run back to the mansion at the edge of the orchard.

"Oh," she says.

She shimmies out of her cloak; it pools around her feet like a curious flower. The flash of silver I saw last time isn't here. She wears a blue dress, the sleeves stopping just above her rounded, scarred elbows. 'The girl without hands,' the women who pick pears every day from dawn till dusk whisper with gleeful malice.

"Keep the cloak," she says. "It's cold tonight—too cold for only a blanket."

My fingers close around the lush, velvet fabric. There it is again, the scent of honeysuckle. My eyes wander. I can't help but quirk my eyebrow when I notice the basket filled with pears she's left at my side. As if I can't pick them for myself.

Her lips lift into a smile. "Consider it a gesture of goodwill. Pears from my orchard, or at least my husband's orchard."

She's married—of course she is. The lady of the estate.

I take one of the pears and dig my nails into its flesh, releasing the crisp, sweet scent into the air. Pears are hard for me to eat, even the ones that fall to the ground and turn mushy. In yet another cruel twist of fate, human experiences keep eluding me, so I've stopped seeking them out. But because she's looking at me expectantly, I bring the fruit to my nose.

Thank you, I mouth.

She smiles again, a midnight sun. "How did you end up here?"

I thought I loved him. I thought he would love me back. Now I don't want to be in the palace or near the ocean when the prince decides to stop waiting for the one who saved him from drowning. When he marries a noble human girl instead. I want to be away from the temptation of slicing his throat as he sleeps.

I try to mouth something about princes and wishes and how I don't want to find out about my sea-foam-demise until it's already upon me, but she's having trouble following my lips. My ever-blistering-bleeding-burning feet are hurting, my stomach painfully rumbles for those pears I can still smell, and she's *so goddamn beautiful.*

"Tomorrow at dusk. Will you be here?" she asks, as if she cares about the answer.

I raise my jutting shoulders. I never stay in one place longer than a few days, yet tomorrow will mark my fourth day in the orchard. Nobody has asked me to stay before, not since the prince.

So I stay. And the girl returns the next day.

"You can look," she says after she's settled herself between the forked roots of my tree. "It's worse when people pretend they cannot see my prosthetics."

I do as I'm told. Her arms seem flexible, the hollow metal sleek and shiny. The forearms taper off into slender, ball-jointed wrists and fingers. The prosthetics tie at her elbows and shoulders with leather straps and buckles she operates with her teeth.

I catch myself wondering if her hands would feel cold or warm against my skin.

"My husband had them made for me." Her voice turns from confident to confidential. "They're useful, of course, but I feel more like myself without them."

I nod toward the house in the distance, illuminated like a lighthouse. I want the gesture to be casual, but my human body betrays me by setting my cheeks aflame.

She touches her flat stomach, a sad smile playing across her lips. "My husband, he's in mourning. Barely leaves the house anymore."

They had a son. She says he was beautiful. He lives among the stars now. An angel has him.

"I know he's in a good place, but I'd give anything to have him back." She digs her bare toes into the moss, her eyes cast downward.

Don't, I want to say. *There's always a catch.* Prayers and wishes, they're tricky like that. Like when I wished for legs, a soul, and the love of my prince.

Like when I wish now, to sit closer to you, reach out and touch your smooth skin and smoother hair.

It's uncanny how easily the creek girl and I slip into a routine. During the day, I work in the orchard, away from the other girls and their gossip. Then, when everyone's gone and the sky is streaked mauve and coral, she comes. Sometimes she brings me things. Soap and twine, paper and charcoal—and food I always refuse. Mostly, we just sit together, in the orchard or by the creek.

It happens slowly. When I saw the prince on the deck of the royal ship, the very first night I rose to the ocean's surface, I fell for him hard and fast. With her, it creeps up on me. When she uses the back of her hand to tuck a lock of russet hair behind my ear. When she says something so unexpected it makes me realize laughing isn't as impossible for me to do as I had once thought. When her usually tranquil face falls, and I hasten to lift the spell of sadness.

I don't want her to mother me like my sisters and grandmother used to. I want her to touch me where nobody else has, in that unfamiliar, skittering place between my legs, even in the hollow where my tongue used to be.

Back in the ocean, I only used my voice for singing—a high, ethereal keen. Everything else I communicated through a flare of gills, stirring of scales, or flick of fins. Now, I have nothing. There are only my useless vocal cords and the dark void of my mouth and chest. Only the sensation of swords going through my legs and of sharp knives cutting my feet—the pain and blood the sea witch spoke about when I gave up my tail, too lovesick to heed her warnings.

I should do the right thing, pack my meager belongings and continue journeying away from the ocean. Instead, I lie awake long after the creek girl is gone, wishing she could read my thoughts and come closer to me, because sometimes, it feels like I'll break apart if I take another step on land. I'll turn into sea foam long before the witch prophesied.

So, every day, anxiety eats away at me as I wait for her to arrive. And every night, her husband stands in the doorway while she walks back to their house with starlight at her heels. He welcomes her inside, an arm around her shoulders, a kiss on her cheek.

She notices me watching the house one evening.

"You can come inside, you know. Let the servants cook something for you. Sleep on a bed for once. My husband would love to meet you."

All three of us sleeping under the same roof... I fix her with a pointed look.

"Fine. Then you could join the worker women in their quarters."

I open and close my fingers, minnow-fast.

She chuckles. "They have a tendency to ramble, but

they're not bad people. There was a girl here once who used to talk with her hands. Sign language, she called it. You could learn it too."

That night, I dream about the prince waiting for the saintly girl he's molded to perfection in his mind, the saviour he doesn't know is me. I dream about the girl I ache for lying in bed with her husband and the ghost of a dead baby between them. I dream about my hands turning into birds capable of words. But for the first time, I don't dream about the ocean.

The sunlight makes our reflections shimmer in the water. It's hard to believe this is the same creek where her two-year-old drowned. Unlike me, she doesn't shy away from pain. She visits the creek to feel closer to him, while I run away; from the ocean, the palace, from everything that hurts me. Too bad I can't run from myself.

Her prosthetics lie between us on the grass. They've left indentations on her skin, red and irritated like a rash. I dip my bare toes in the stream, my torn skirt hitched up around my knees, pink rivulets of blood drifting around the river bend.

I miss the sea, but not the salt and the memories. At least here, the water is sweet and clear. I can almost forget who I am and where I've come from.

"Do you think I'm incomplete?" she asks, interrupting her prayer about lost children.

My eyes widen, head jerking from side to side, silent litany of *nonono* dropping from my lips.

She smiles. "I know you wouldn't think that." Sadness pools in the corners of her mouth. "So why do you consider *yourself* incomplete?"

I stagger to my feet, blood and water everywhere. If I had a tongue, it'd be so heavy in my mouth. Instantly, my vision blackens, dizziness dragging me in a downward spiral, but I can't let it show.

How does this girl I can't talk to know me better than anyone I knew?

She's told me about phantom pain before. I can feel it now in every inch of my body, old and new, mermaid and human.

She comes up behind me and hugs me, presses her chest against my trembling back.

"I understand. I was like you once, stubborn, angry, and confused. I left my family and wealth behind to prove I could survive in the world on my own, that I was *enough*. It's not an easy process, but you'll get there, I know you will."

Her touch feels worse, and yet more wonderful than I had imagined on all those nights beneath the stars. How do I explain that she's gold and light and honeysuckle, and I'm blood and emptiness and salty, rotten fish tang?

But maybe she sees something in me in despite — or maybe because — of all that I am. Something she's lived through before, something worthy of her love.

And maybe I can learn to see it too.

"How long has it been since the last time you ate?" she asks one evening as the dying sun paints everything crimson.

Once again, it's as if she's reading my mind. I used to be strong and lithe, but now I'm barely a slip of a girl. The hunger keeps combating the emptiness inside. I can't remember the last time I was full.

I shrug and mouth, *You?*

She avoids my eyes. "My husband takes most of his meals in bed, and I don't like eating alone in the dining room. I can feel the servants' pity."

So, her husband isn't doing any better. My heart flails and flounders in my chest. Of course. This is why her visits to the orchard last longer every day—it's the only explanation.

The trees around us are laden with fruit. I climb up the sturdier branches until I reach the top, where the pears are round, unmarred. Despite the pain, my legs are sure and agile.

I used to dance for the prince, in the palace by the ocean. He said I was the best dancer he had ever seen, clapped, and laughed while I left blood on the sparkling marble floors. Another dance, another piece of me gone. And if—*when*—the prince weds another girl, dissolving into sea foam will be my final dance.

"Get down here," the creek girl chides, looking up the length of the trunk. "You think I can't tell this is hurting you?"

I fall back to the ground, offer her the fattest, prettiest pear.

She considers. "I'll take it only if you eat it too."

Eating is neither easy nor pretty for me. I have to tilt my head back like a bird gobbling up a worm, use my throat muscles to push the food deeper. The process often involves silent heaves of my chest and drool dripping past my lips. Solid foods scrape my throat like fishhooks. At the palace—when the prince still cared about me the way one cares about a pet—I drank viscous pastes made of honey and ground oats. But no one worries about how I eat anymore, nor how I survive on land.

I mime this as best as I can.

She scoffs. "Who cares about pretty?"

To illustrate her point, she leans down and bites unabashedly into the pear in my hand, the juices running down her chin. She wipes her mouth on the shoulder of her fine dress and laughs.

"Your turn," she announces.

I lock eyes with her as I bring the pear to my mouth. I trace her teeth marks, the act sending a tingle through my body, down into my toes. She doesn't recoil or look revolted as we share the pear. When only the seeds and stem remain, we lie down side by side underneath the oldest tree where we first met. Has it only been a month?

She tells me stories of sea and forest, earth and sky. The

praying mantises hop around in the grass. The stars blink above us, her rapt audience. I feel like crying, but I'm scared of the taste of salt. If I start crying now, I'll never stop.

I screw my eyes shut to capture the wetness. When I open them again, she's on her side, smiling at me - soft, tender. Mischievous. And then her lips are on mine, her tongue charting the inside of my mouth. I shouldn't be able to taste anything, but I swear the kiss carries the tart sweetness from the pear, the freshness of the creek, the crispness of the night air.

When I regain control of my body, I draw back, yanking my head in the direction of the house, but she seems unperturbed.

"Did I ever tell you how my husband and I met?"

I glower.

She laughs, high and clear as a bell. "I have a feeling you'll like the story."

And so she tells me about arriving at the orchard with only the clothes on her back, asking for a job, and getting laughed at by the other workers. The rumours about her were only surpassed by the whispers about her future husband, the mild-mannered, orphaned estate owner who preferred the company of men over women. They soon became friends, decided to marry and offer each other a good, safe life.

"So, will you finally accept my invitation and come inside?" she asks with a glinting smile. "My husband is curious about the girl who's stolen my heart."

I laugh, my chest shaking with both mirth and astonishment.

I pull her close and kiss her. The taste like a prayer finally being answered.

Acknowledgements

WE'D LIKE TO FIRST and foremost thank *you*. Thank you for picking up this book and reading these wonderful stories. Giving these writers a platform is so important to us, so do make sure to check out their social media.

The charity we are partnered with is Coram Beanstalk, and we want to thank them for being so magnificent at all the hard work they do. If you'd like to know more about them, please turn the page. You'll have also donated money to their cause by purchasing this book – we send a portion of our profits to aid in the work they do.

We'd also like to take a moment to reach out and thank our friends and loved ones for supporting us while we went on this crazy adventure. Jake Reed, Luella Williamson, Lizzie Gilholme and Josie Deacon – thank you for your unconditional and unending emotional and creative support.

Thank you to our lovely indiegogo supporters, in particular Kirsty Frith, Ruthie Clark, Stephanie Wasek, Jack Ibbotson and Maryann Troche.

Finally, we (Lucy and Kristel) want to thank our wonderful creative team. Thank you so much to Josie

Deacon and Molly Llewellyn for putting in your time and efforts to this project and helping to bring it to fruition.

Dancing Bear Books

DANCING BEAR BOOKS is an independent press based in the UK. We were founded on the basis that we believe everyone should be able to tell and read their stories. We want to fill bookshelves with tales we believe are missing from literature today.

Creating a space for diverse voices and stories has never been more important. Nobody should be made to feel as if the space they take up in the world is wasted on them, we want our books to be a proud coat of arms that carves out room for those voices.

———

www.dancingbearbooks.co.uk
Instagram @dancingbearbooks
Twitter @dancingbearbook
Facebook @dancingbearbooks

Coram Beanstalk

CORAM BEANSTALK recruits, trains and supports volunteers to provide one-to-one literacy support in early years settings and primary schools to children who have fallen behind with their reading.

Their volunteers transform the lives of the children they support, turning them into confident, passionate and able readers.

———

www.beanstalkcharity.org.uk
Instagram @beanstalkreads
Twitter @beanstalkreads
Facebook @beanstalkreads

Some lived happily ever after, and some did not. But each lived a life of bravery and courage.

The End.

Dancing Bear Books
Coming to a bookshelf near you:

WOMXN
The Tarot Deck Collection: Classics